THE GIRL
WHO READS
ON
THE MÉTRO

THE GIRL WHO READS ON THE MÉTRO

CHRISTINE FÉRET-FLEURY

TRANSLATED FROM THE FRENCH
BY ROS SCHWARTZ

FLATIRON
BOOKS
NEW YORK

THE GIRL WHO READS ON THE MÉTRO. Copyright © 2017 by Christine Féret-Fleury. Translation copyright © 2019 by Ros Schwartz. All rights reserved. Printed in the United States of America. For information, address Flatiron Books, 120 Broadway, New York, NY 10271.

www.flatironbooks.com

Designed by Anna Gorovoy

The Library of Congress Cataloging-in-Publication Data is available on request.

ISBN 978-1-250-31542-7 (hardcover)
ISBN 978-1-250-31543-4 (ebook)

Our books may be purchased in bulk for promotional, educational, or business use. Please contact your local bookseller or the Macmillan Corporate and Premium Sales Department at 1-800-221-7945, extension 5442, or by email at MacmillanSpecialMarkets@macmillan.com.

Originally published in France in 2017 as
La Fille qui lisait dans le métro by Editions Denoël

First U.S. Edition: October 2019

10 9 8 7 6 5 4 3 2 1

I have always imagined that Paradise will be a kind of library.
—JORGE LUIS BORGES, "THE ALEPH"

THE GIRL
WHO READS
ON
THE MÉTRO

The man in the green hat always got on at Bercy, always via the doors at the front of the compartment, and exited via the same doors at La Motte-Picquet–Grenelle, exactly seventeen minutes later. That was on days when the stops, warning signals, and clanging were regular, the days that weren't exceptionally overcrowded, when there were no accidents, terror alerts, or strikes, and no unscheduled stops to regulate the trains. Ordinary days. The days when you feel as though you're a cog in a well-oiled machine, a huge mechanical body in which each person has their place and their part to play, willingly or not.

On those days, Juliette would take refuge behind her butterfly-framed sunglasses and her chunky scarf knitted by Granny Adrienne in 1975 for her daughter. The two-and-a-half-meter scarf was a faded blue, the color of distant peaks at seven o'clock on a summer's eve, not just anywhere but in the Pyrenean town of Prades gazing toward Mount Canigou. And Juliette would sit wondering whether her existence in this world was any more precious than that of the spider she'd drowned that morning in her shower.

She didn't like doing that—aiming the jet at the small, black, hairy creature and watching out of the corner of her eye as the spindly legs flailed in panic and then abruptly folded in on the body. Then the spider would whirl around, as light and inconsequential as a wisp of wool plucked from her favorite sweater, until it was sucked down the plughole which she immediately stopped up, jamming in the plug.

Serial murder. Every day, the spiders crawled up, emerging from the pipes after a wobbly climb. Were they always the same ones that, after being flushed down into the murky depths—the bowels of the city like a vast reservoir of teeming, stinking life—unfolded themselves, came back to life, and embarked on another ascent invariably destined to fail? It was hard to imagine. Juliette saw herself as a pitiless but negligent divinity, too busy most of the time to fulfill her role, intermittently guarding the gates of Hell. What were the spiders hoping for once their feet were on dry land, so to speak? What journey had they decided to undertake, and with what purpose?

The man in the green hat could perhaps have given her the answer if Juliette had dared ask him. Every morning, he would open his briefcase and take out a book covered in thin, almost transparent paper, also of a greenish hue. He'd unfold its corners with slow, deliberate movements, then slide a finger between two pages already separated by a strip of the same paper, and begin reading.

The title of the book was: *A History of Insects Useful to Man, Animals and the Arts, with a Supplement on How to Destroy Pests.*

He would caress the mottled leather cover, its spine decorated with thin gold lettering, the title standing out against a red background.

He'd open it, bring it closer to his face, and sniff it, his eyes half-closed.

He'd read two or three pages, no more, like a food-lover eating cream pastries with a tiny silver spoon. A happy, enigmatic smile would appear on his face—the kind that Juliette, fascinated, imagined as that of the Cheshire Cat in *Alice in Wonderland*.

That smile faded at Cambronne, giving way to an expression of rueful disappointment; he would then refold the paper, put the book back in his briefcase, and snap it shut. And stand up. Not once did he look at Juliette, who, sitting opposite him—or standing, huddled against the shiny pole polished each day by hundreds of gloved or ungloved palms—devoured him with her eyes. He would patter off, very upright in his overcoat buttoned up to the neck, with his hat cocked over his left eyebrow.

Without that hat, without that smile, without that briefcase in which he shut away his treasure, Juliette probably wouldn't have recognized him. He was a man like any other, neither good-looking nor ugly, neither attractive nor repulsive.

A little portly, of uncertain age, or rather, a certain age, to speak in clichés.

A man.

Or rather, a reader.

Bees, silkworms, mealybugs, crayfish, wood lice, blister beetles, leeches . . .

"What are you on about?"

Juliette, who was humming, jumped.

"Oh! Nothing. A sort of counting rhyme . . . I was trying to remember the names . . ."

"I've received the energy performance certificate for the Boulevard Voltaire apartment," said Chloe, who wasn't listening. "Have you got the folder?"

Juliette nodded after a moment. She was still thinking about the man with the green book, about insects, about the spider she'd drowned that morning.

"Give it to me. I'll file it," she said.

She pivoted her chair, pulled a binder from the shelves that covered an entire wall of the office, and slipped the documents inside. The binder, she noted, was piss yellow. How sad that was. The whole bulging wall, bristling with labels coming unstuck at the corners, looked as if it were about to collapse on top of her like a mudslide. Juliette closed her eyes, imagining the swashing sound, the gas bubbles popping on the surface—and the smell. She pinched her nose hard to quell her mounting nausea.

"What's up?" asked Chloe.

Juliette shrugged.

"Are you pregnant?" her colleague pressed her.

"Of course not. I was just wondering how you cope with working opposite that . . . the color's so disgusting."

Chloe stared at her wide-eyed.

"Dis-gus-ting," she repeated slowly. "You're bonkers. They're just binders. They're ugly, I agree, but . . . are you sure you're okay?"

Juliette drummed her fingers on her desk in a jerky rhythm: *Bees, silkworms, mealybugs, crayfish, wood lice, blister beetles, leeches . . .*

"I'm fine," she replied. "What do you read on the Métro?"

2

There was the old lady, the math student, the amateur ornithologist, the gardener, and the woman in love—at least Juliette assumed she was in love from her slight breathlessness and the tiny tears that formed on her eyelashes when she was three-quarters of the way through whichever romantic novel she was devouring. They were fat books, dog-eared from being read over and over again. Sometimes on the cover there was an illustration of a couple locked in an embrace on a bloodred background, or lace suggestive of a bra. The torso of a naked man, the small of a back, a crumpled bedsheet or a pair of cuff links, sober punctuation of the title underlined by a horizontal leather-sheathed riding crop . . . and the tears that welled up in the young woman's eyes, always around page 247 (Juliette had checked by glancing covertly at her neighbor), then rolled slowly down toward her jawline, while her eyelids closed, and an involuntary sigh made her plump breasts swell in their overly modest little top. *Why page 247?* wondered

Juliette as she stared after an unfurled umbrella making its way down the platform at Dupleix, protecting from the downpour an entire family whose legs alone were visible—little legs in brown corduroy, long denim-clad legs, slim legs in striped tights. What was happening at that point, what sudden emotion was sparked, what heartbreak, what anguish, what shudder of pleasure or abandon?

Pensive, she drummed her fingers on the cover of her own book, which she no longer opened very often, so absorbed was she in watching other people. The coffee-stained paperback with a broken spine was transferred from bag to bag, from Tuesday's big shoulder bag—the day when Juliette did her food shopping after work—to the little handbag she used on Fridays, when she went to the cinema. A postcard slipped between pages 32 and 33 hadn't shifted for over a week. The landscape it depicted, a mountain village in the distance above a patchwork of fields in various hues of brown, she now associated with the old lady, the one who always flicked through the same collection of recipes and occasionally smiled as if the description of a dish reminded her of a moment of youthful madness, and who sometimes shut the book, placed her ringless hand on top of it, and stared out the window at the barges on the Seine or the roofs glistening in the rain. The back-cover blurb was in Italian, centered above a photo of two plump bell peppers, a fat fennel bulb, and a mozzarella ball in which a horn-handled knife had made a straight incision.

Bees, silkworms, mealybugs, crayfish, wood lice, blister beetles, leeches . . . *Carciofi, arancie, pomodori, fagiolini, zucchini . . . Crostate, lombatine di cervo, gamberi al gratin . . .* Butterfly words that fluttered around the packed compartment before settling on Juliette's fingertips. She found the image cheesy, but it was the only one that came to mind. Why butterflies, anyway? Why not fireflies, winking for a few seconds before dying? But when had she seen fireflies? Never, as a matter of fact. There weren't any fireflies left, she feared. Only memories. Memories of her grandmother, the one who'd knitted her scarf. And who looked a bit like the old lady with the recipe book—same pale, serene face, same strong-looking hands, with stubby fingers adorned with just one ring, the thick wedding band which over the years had dug into her flesh and made a permanent mark. Her wrinkled, blotchy skin covered the ring; her body swallowed up the symbol, became deformed by it.

"Fireflies," she used to say. "Fireflies are fallen stars. I was still so young that I wasn't allowed to stay up, and the summer evenings were so long! For at least two hours the slits in the shutters let the light in. It crept softly across the rug and climbed up the bars of my bed; and then, suddenly, the brass bed knob began to shine. I knew that I was missing the best bit, that moment when the sun sinks into the sea, when it becomes like wine, or like blood. So, I'd knot my nightdress, like this, around my waist, nice and tight. And I'd climb down, holding on to the trellis. A right little monkey. And I'd run to the end of the field, to the spot from which you could see the sea. Then, when it was properly dark, I'd perch on the gate that was always left open, behind the silkworm farm . . . that's where I saw them. They arrived out of nowhere. Or they came out of the ground. I never found out. Silent, suspended in mid-air, settling on blades of grass . . . I didn't move a muscle. I didn't even dare breathe. I was surrounded by stars."

The Métro slowed down. Sèvres-Lecourbe. Three more stops, or four, depending on the day and on Juliette's mood. Squeal of metal, signal. All of a sudden, she leapt up and ran out, just as the doors were about to close, and her jacket got caught as they slammed shut. She yanked it out and was left standing rooted to the platform, slightly breathless, as the train pulled away. In the morning grayness, a few shapes muffled in heavy coats were heading for the exit. On a February morning, who walked for the pleasure of roaming the streets aimlessly, looking up, observing the shapes of the clouds, or out of sheer curiosity? No one. People went from the cozy warmth of their apartments to their overheated offices, drank coffee, yawning as they commented on the day's tasks, the gossip, the news—always depressing. There was only one street to cross between the station where Juliette alighted each day and the door of the estate agency where she worked. A flight of steps, a stretch of pavement, then, on the left, the windows of a dry cleaner, a tobacconist's, and a kebab shop. In the tobacconist's window, a plastic Christmas tree, still decked with tinsel and shiny paper chains, was beginning to gather dust.

Juliette wanted to see something different. She walked over

to the map of the neighborhood at the far end of the station: if she took the first street on her right, then turned right again at the second intersection, it wouldn't take more than ten minutes to get to work. A little walk would warm her up. She wouldn't be late—well, hardly. In any case, Chloe would open up. That girl was obsessively punctual, and either way, Monsieur Bernard, the manager, never arrived before half past nine.

Juliette set off along the street at a rapid pace, then forced herself to slow down. She must get out of the habit of forging straight ahead, her eyes fixed on the goal. Nothing exciting awaited her, nothing: documents to complete and file away, a long list of tedious formalities, a viewing or two perhaps. On good days. To think she'd chosen this profession for the excitement!

As for dealing with people, the ad she'd replied to had promised that this meant building relationships with them and reading their hopes and dreams in their eyes, then finding them a nest where those dreams could unfurl, where the fearful would regain their confidence, where the depressed would smile once more, where children would grow up sheltered from the strong winds that batter and uproot, where the elderly and the weary could peacefully wait for death.

She clearly remembered her first viewing, a thirtysomething couple in a hurry. She'd suggested a coffee before they went into the apartment building. "I need to get to know you better, clarify your expectations," she'd stated with a confidence that she was a long way from feeling at that moment.

Clarify your expectations, she thought that sounded good—she'd read it in the booklet given to each member of staff by the management—but the man had stared at her, one eyebrow raised, then tapped his watch meaningfully. The woman was checking her messages on her smartphone; she hadn't looked up, not even as they went up the stairs, while Juliette, frozen, had reeled off the features she had memorized the previous evening: ashlar and the charm of the Haussmann-style architecture, you'll notice the floor tiles in the lobby, restored to match the original sections, total peace and quiet, there's an elevator to the fourth floor, and look at the thickness of the stair carpeting. Her voice sounded as if it was coming from very far away, ridiculously high-pitched, the voice of a little girl playing at being a grown-up. She felt sorry for herself and had a sudden, absurd urge to burst into tears. The couple tore through the apartment, a two-bedroom overlooking an interior courtyard, while she tried to keep up with them. The words blew away, tumbled over each other: lovely high ceilings, elegant fireplace moldings, lots of cupboard space, diamond-design parquet floors, which are very rare, the option of creating an additional bedroom or office by putting in a mezzanine ... They weren't listening, didn't look at each other, didn't ask anything. Valiantly, she'd tried to question them: Do you play the piano? Do you have any children or ... ? Receiving no answers, she'd stumbled over a ray of light slanting across a parquet floor tile covered in a fine layer of dust, her voice farther and farther away, so weak that it was impossible for anyone to hear it: a dual-aspect apartment, very light, the sun in the kitchen from nine o'clock in the morning . . . They had already left, so she ran after them. In the street she'd given her card to the man, who'd put it in his pocket without looking at it.

She already knew she would never see them again.

A seagull's cry brought Juliette back down to earth. She stopped and looked up. Wings outstretched, the bird was circling above her head. A low cloud passed beneath it, and its beak and body disappeared; all that remained were the tips of its wings and its cry, which bounced off the high walls. A gust of wind whipped Juliette's face, sending her reeling back. It had a sobering effect and she looked about her. The street was dismal, empty, lined with apartment buildings streaked with long trails of damp, the plaster flaking off. What the hell was she doing here? She shuddered, buried her face in her big scarf, and set off again.

"Zaide!"

The voice seemed to be coming from very high up, but the little girl who was running toward her ignored it; agile and spirited, she ducked between Juliette's legs and an overturned recycling bin spewing plastic waste, gathered her skinny limbs and started hopping about on the slippery pavement again.

Juliette turned to watch her skip off, skirt swirling, little pea-green sweater, two dancing braids . . . and her gaze fell on a high, rusted metal door, wedged open with a book . . . a book.

In tall blue letters, on an enameled metal doorplate straight out of a World War II film, were the words: BOOKS UNLIMITED.

Juliette took three steps forward, reached out, and gingerly touched the pages swollen from the damp. She ran her tongue over her upper lip. Seeing a book wedged between two metal doors hurt her almost more than drowning a spider. Gently, she leaned her shoulder against one of the double doors and heaved; the book slid a little farther down. She caught it and, with her shoulder still to the door, raised the book to her face.

She had always loved the smell of books, especially when she bought them secondhand. New books had different smells, too, depending on the paper and glue used, but they said nothing of the hands that had held them, the houses that had been their home; they had no story of their own yet, separate from the one they told—a parallel story, hazy, secret.

Some smelled musty, others exuded the clinging aroma of curry, tea, or dried flowers; sometimes the pages had grease stains, or a long blade of grass that had served as a bookmark on a summer afternoon, turned to dust; phrases underlined or notes in the margin constituting a fragmented diary, a sketchy biography, sometimes bearing witness to indignation, or a separation.

This one smelled of the street—a mixture of rust and smoke, of guano and burnt tires. But also, surprisingly, of mint. Stalks fell out of the fold, dropped soundlessly to the ground, and the fragrance became even more intense.

"Zaide!"

The voice shouted again, a galloping sound; Juliette felt a warm little body bang into her.

"Excuse me."

The voice, surprisingly deep for a child, sounded shocked. Juliette looked down and met a pair of brown eyes, so dark that the dilated pupils seemed to fill the irises.

"This is my house," said the little girl.

"May I come in?" Juliette whispered.

"Of course."

Awkwardly, Juliette stepped sideways and the heavy door began to close. The little girl pushed it with both hands.

"That's why Papa always leaves a book there," she explained patiently. "The handle's too stiff for me."

"But why a book?"

The question burst out like a criticism. Juliette felt herself blush, which hadn't happened to her for a long time—especially not in front of a ten-year-old pip-squeak.

Zaide—what a pretty name—shrugged.

"Oh, them! He says they're 'cuckoos.' That's funny, isn't it?

Like the birds. They've got the same pages repeated three or four times, they haven't been made right, you see? You can't read them. Well, not really. Show me that one."

The girl leaned forward, closed her eyes, and sniffed.

"I tried to read it. It's a stupid story, about a girl who meets a boy. She hates him and then she loves him, but then he hates her and . . . I was so bored that I put mint leaves in it so that at least it would smell nice."

"That's a lovely idea," said Juliette softly.

"Do you want to come in? Are you one of the *passeurs*? I've never seen you before."

Passeurs? Juliette shook her head. The word evoked images from a black-and-white film: hazy shapes bent double running through tunnels or crawling under barbed wire as the *passeurs* smuggled Jews out of the German-occupied zone to safety, young women on bicycles carrying Resistance pamphlets in their saddlebags and smiling with feigned innocence at a German soldier wearing a gray-green salad bowl helmet. Images seen hundreds of times at the cinema or on TV, so familiar that you sometimes forgot the horrors they represented.

"So, do you want to be one?" Zaide went on. "It's easy. Come on, let's go and see my father."

Once again, Juliette shook her head. Then her gaze left the little girl's face and lighted on the doorplate with the mysterious but simple wording. BOOKS UNLIMITED. Such a curious name. Books know neither limits nor borders, except sometimes of the language in which they're written—so why . . . ?

She could feel her mind wandering, even though she was aware that the clock was ticking and she had to leave, get away from this street and return as soon as possible to the neon lighting of her office at the back of the agency, the musty odor of property files and client files, Chloe's nonstop chatter and Monsieur Bernard's cough, loose or dry depending on the season, the fourth viewing for a retired couple who couldn't make up their minds between a house in suburban Milly-la-Forêt or a one-bedroom apartment near Porte d'Italie.

"Come on," Zaide urged her again.

She took Juliette's hand and pulled her into the courtyard, then carefully put the book back to prop open the door.

"That's the office, over there across the courtyard, with the glass door. Just knock. I'm going upstairs."

"Don't you go to school?" asked Juliette instinctively.

"There's a case of chicken pox in my class," replied the girl self-importantly. "We've all been sent home; I've even got a note for my father. Don't you believe me?"

Her little round face had creased into a worried frown. The tip of her tongue peeked out from between her lips, as pink and smooth as a marzipan flower.

Of course Juliette believed her.

"That's okay then. It's just you're all so suspicious," Zaide concluded with a shrug.

She spun around and again her braids bounced on her shoulders. Her hair was dark brown, with a honey sheen when the sun caught it; each of her braids was as thick as her delicate wrist.

While she raced up the steps of a metal staircase that led to a long gallery running the length of the first floor of the building—probably a former factory—Juliette made her way hesitantly toward the glass door. She didn't know exactly why she'd followed the little girl and was now obeying her order— thinking about it, was it an order? Or a piece of advice? In any case, this was utter madness: she was already late, she knew it without needing to look at her watch. A fine drizzle was now falling and gently stinging her face, prompting her to seek warmth, a temporary shelter. After all, she had nothing urgent to do that morning . . . she could always say her washing machine was on the blink. It had been acting up for months. She had even talked at length to Monsieur Bernard about it, and he'd insisted on explaining to her the merits of the different brands. He maintained that the German ones were the best, so much more reliable, he claimed, and even offered to go with her the following Saturday to a store he knew: the manager was a distant cousin, a trustworthy man who would advise her well.

The glazed door sparkled, reflecting a section of sky—and in the depths of the room, a light was on.

Juliette raised her hand and knocked.

4.

"It's open!"

A man's voice. Slightly muffled, husky even, tinged with an indefinable accent. At the far end of the room, a long shape unfurled. As she pushed open the door, Juliette saw a mountain of boxes, the top ones placed slightly askew, which began to wobble. "Watch out!" she yelled. Too late: the boxes crashed to the floor, sending up a cloud of dust. Juliette began to choke, and covered her mouth and nose with her hand. She heard a curse, which she didn't understand, and glimpsed movement—the man had fallen to his knees. She saw he was dark-haired, dressed in black, quite thin, and was rubbing his eyes.

"I don't believe it! I'd sorted them all out . . . Will you help me?"

His tone, this time, was imperious. At a loss for words, Juliette nodded and moved toward the light, where the voice had come from. The man was alone. He waved his arms around, his too-short sleeves revealing bony wrists, and, now that the dust had settled a little, she could see his profile: clean, almost sharp, his nose as straight as that of a Greek god, or of the warriors on the Knossos frescoes. She'd spent two weeks on Crete the previous summer and she had often seen them since, in her dreams, brandishing javelins and running headlong into the assault, their long, almond-shaped eyes filled with visions of glory and immortality.

"Of course," she mumbled, not certain whether he'd heard her.

He gathered up the scattered books, flailing around like a clumsy swimmer. The books were thigh high, lying higgledy-piggledy, the covers sliding over one another, fanning out, some books fallen open. All of a sudden, she thought she heard the hum of a chickadee flying out of a bush.

When she was directly in front of him, he looked up and voiced his dismay with childlike simplicity.

"I can't remember how I'd sorted these. By subject and by country, perhaps. Or by genre." He added, as if in apology: "I'm very absentminded. My daughter's always scolding me. She says a bird flew off with my brain a long time ago."

"Little Zaide?" asked Juliette, already crouching down, her hands moving among the pages. "Is she your daughter?"

Before Juliette was spread an almost complete set of Zola's novels: *The Fortune of the Rougons, The Kill, The Sin of Abbé Mouret, A Love Story, Pot Luck, Nana, The Masterpiece* . . . She gathered them up and made a neat pile on the floor, beside the sea of scattered books.

"Have you met her?"

"Yes, she's the one who invited me in."

"I should tell her to be more careful."

"Do I look so dangerous?"

Above the pile of Zolas, a man's face with a pencil mustache was arrogantly staring at her. She deciphered the title: *Bel Ami*.

"Maupassant," she said. "And here's Daudet. Naturalist novels. Maybe you'd tried to classify them by literary genre . . ."

He wasn't listening.

"No, you don't look dangerous," he admitted after a moment's thought. "Are you a bookseller? Or a teacher? Librarian, maybe?"

"No, nothing like that, I . . . I work in property. But my grandfather was a bookseller. I used to love his shop when I was little. I loved helping him. I adored the smell of books . . ."

The smell of books . . . it would hit her even before she walked into the bookshop, the moment she caught sight of the narrow window where her grandfather only ever displayed one volume at a time, usually an open art book on a stand, and each day he would turn one page. People stopped, she recalled, to look at the picture of the day: a little Jacob van Ruisdael, a portrait by Jean-Baptiste Greuze, a seascape by Nicolas Ozanne . . .

For the little girl, and later adolescent, the shop was the palace out of the *One Thousand and One Nights*, her refuge on wet Wednesday afternoons, which she spent arranging the new arrivals on the shelves or reading in the stockroom. A passionate book lover, always on the lookout for rare editions, her grandfather bought entire collections of secondhand books, most of which were piled up in tall crates to the right of the door. Rummaging through these treasures, Juliette had discovered not only the classics of children's literature, but also works by authors who'd gone out of fashion: Charles Morgan, Daphne du Maurier, Barbey d'Aurevilly, and a whole host of English female novelists, including Rosamond Lehmann. She devoured Agatha Christie novels like sweets . . .

The voice of the man in black brought her abruptly back to the present.

"Here, take these here. Now I remember I didn't know where to put them. I suppose that means they're ready to leave."

Juliette instinctively opened her hands to take the pile of books he was holding out to her, then echoed, surprised: "Ready to leave?"

"Yes. That's why you're here, isn't it? You want to be a *passeur*? Ordinarily I should have asked you some questions first. I'd made a list, over there"—he pointed vaguely at the desk strewn with papers and articles cut out of newspapers—"but I can never find it when I need it. I can offer you a cup of coffee, though."

"I . . . no, thank you, I have to—"

"But I still need to explain to you how we operate . . . we, I mean they, because I . . . well, it's a bit complicated. I don't go out." He got up, deftly using his hands for support, stepped over the boxes, and made his way to the back of the room where, on a little table, stood a sort of metal contraption, as well as cups and a tin with the old-fashioned inscription: BIS-CUITS LEFÈVRE-UTILE.

"It's a percolator of my own invention," he said with his back to Juliette. "It works on the principle of the pellet stove . . . do you see what I mean?"

"Not really," mumbled Juliette, who felt most definitely she was being drawn into the realm of the absurd.

She was late. Very late now. Chloe must already have called her cell phone—switched off—to find out whether she was ill. Monsieur Bernard would have walked into his glass-walled office—on the left as you entered the agency—removed his coat and hung it in the cupboard, checking that the shoulders were perfectly level on the hanger with its cedarwood disc to keep the moths away. He would have switched on his personal coffee maker, placed two sugar lumps in his Limoges porcelain cup rimmed with two thin bands of gold, the sole vestige of his mother's coffee service, he'd once told her. A charming woman but a scatterbrain, she'd broken all the others, even throwing one at his father's head when she'd found out he was having an affair with his secretary—a classic scenario. The telephone would have already rung a couple of times, Chloe taking the calls. What time was it? Juliette glanced anxiously at the window, then inhaled the aroma of coffee and forgot her guilt. The man was energetically turning the handle of a wooden coffee grinder. He hummed, as if he'd forgotten she was there. She felt, rather than heard, the tune swirl around her fleetingly before fading away.

"My name's Soliman," he said, turning to face her. "What's yours?"

"My father used to love Mozart," he said after a while when they were drinking, slowly, a thick, black, almost syrupy coffee. "He named my sister and me after characters in the opera *Zaide*. My daughter is also called Zaide."

"What about your mother? Was she okay with that?"

Juliette, aware of her blunder, turned red and put her cup down.

"I'm sorry. Sometimes I say whatever comes into my head. It's none of my business."

"There's no harm done," he replied with the ghost of a smile that softened his sharp features. "My mother died very young. But for a long time, she hadn't really been with us. Absent . . . in a way."

Without offering any further explanation, he let his gaze wander over the boxes piled up against the partitions, neatly stacked, almost nested—a second wall, insulating the little room from the light and noise outside.

"Have you heard of the principle of releasing books into the wild?" he went on after a few moments' silence. "An American, Ron Hornbaker, created, or rather developed, the concept of BookCrossing in 2001. Turn the whole world into a library . . . a lovely idea, don't you think? You leave a book in a public place—a station, park bench, cinema—someone picks it up, reads it, then releases it elsewhere a few days or weeks later."

He pressed his hands together under his chin, forming an almost perfect triangle.

"What was needed was a way of tracking the books that had been 'released,' following their journey and allowing readers to share their impressions. Hence the BookCrossing website, where each book is registered. It is given an ID which must be included on a label on the cover, with the website URL. Anyone picking up a book can register the date and place where they found it, add an opinion or a review—"

"Is that what you do?" interrupted Juliette.

"Not exactly."

He stood up and went over to the piles of books reconstructed by Juliette as best she could. He took a book from each one.

"Here, we have a fairly random assortment of potential reading. Tolstoy's *War and Peace*. *The Sorrow of Angels* by Jón Kalman Stefánsson. *Suite Française* by Irène Némirovsky. *Winter's End* by Jean-Claude Mourlevat. *Nothing Holds Back the Night* by Delphine de Vigan. *Lancelot, the Knight of the Cart* by Chrétien de Troyes. The next *passeur* who comes into this room will have the responsibility of passing on all these books."

"Responsibility?" asked Juliette.

"They won't release them into the wild or leave them on a train. In other words, they won't leave it to chance for the books to find their readers."

"But how—?"

"The *passeur* has to choose a reader. Someone they will have watched, even followed, until they are able to intuit the book that person needs. Make no mistake, it's a very demanding task. You don't allocate a book as a challenge, on a whim, to upset or provoke. My best *passeurs* have a tremendous capacity for empathy: they feel, in their very bones, the frustrations and resentments that build up deep in a body which, at first glance, looks no different from any other body. Actually, I should say my best *passeur*, singular, because the other one left us very recently."

He put the books down and turned around to pick up, delicately, between two fingers, a photo enlarged to A4 format.

"I wanted to put this on the wall of this office. But she wouldn't have liked that. She was a self-effacing woman, quiet, secretive even. I never found out exactly where she came from. She just appeared one day, like you. Nor do I know why she decided to end her life."

Juliette felt a lump in her throat. The walls of books seemed to be closing in on her, compact and menacing.

"You mean she—?"

"Yes. She committed suicide two days ago."

He nudged the photo across the table toward Juliette. It was a black-and-white shot, slightly grainy, the details blurred by the distance and the poor quality of the print; but she immediately recognized the woman with the thickset body, bundled up in a winter coat, in three-quarter view.

It was the woman with the cookery book who rode Line 6 of the Métro, the one who often looked out with a mysterious, expectant smile.

"I'm so sorry . . . how stupid of me!"

After the fourth or fifth time that Soliman repeated these words, he brought Juliette a box of tissues, another cup of coffee, and a plate—not very clean—onto which he tipped the contents of the tin of biscuits.

"Did you know her?"

"Yes," she managed to reply. "Well, no. She took the same Métro line as I did in the morning. It's true I didn't see her yesterday or the day before. I should have guessed . . . I should have done something for her . . ."

He moved behind her and clumsily rubbed her shoulders. Surprisingly, she found his rough, firm hands comforting.

"No, you shouldn't have. You couldn't have done anything. Look, I'm sorry, very sorry . . ."

Juliette began to laugh nervously.

"Stop saying that."

She straightened up, blinking back her tears. The little room seemed to have shrunk even more, as if the walls of books had taken a step forward into the room. Which was impossible, of course. As impossible as the curve she seemed to see above her head: Were the books in the top row really leaning toward her, their hard backs ready to whisper words of comfort?

Juliette shook her head and stood up, brushing the cookie crumbs from her skirt. They'd been soggy, with a strange taste—too much cinnamon, probably. Soliman hadn't eaten any. The clouds of steam still rising from the percolator—which at regular intervals made a slight clicking sound—formed a veil in front of his face, blurring his features. She had stared at him covertly, looking away when his eyes met hers. When he'd come over and stood behind her, she'd felt relieved. It seemed to her that she had never seen such black eyebrows, such sad eyes, despite the permanent smile that softened the hard outline of his mouth. It was a face that made her think at the same time of storms, of victory and decline. How old could he be?

"I really must go," she said, more to convince herself than for his benefit.

"But you'll come back."

It wasn't a question. He held out the parcel of books, which he'd fastened with a canvas strap. Like in the past, she thought, when children carried schoolbooks—rigid, heavy bundles that dug into their backs as they walked. She wasn't surprised; she couldn't imagine him using a plastic bag.

"Yes. I'll come back."

Wedging the books under her arm, she turned her back to him and made her way over to the door. Her hand on the knob, she stopped.

"Do you ever read love stories?" she asked without turning around.

"This will surprise you," he answered. "Yes, sometimes."

"What happens on page 247?"

There was a pause. He appeared to be thinking about her question. Or perhaps dredging up a memory. Then he said: "On page 247, all seems lost. It's the best moment, you know."

Standing in the crowded compartment the next morning, Juliette felt the canvas bag she was wearing over her shoulder digging into her, just between her ribs and her left hip. The books with their sharp corners were trying to get inside her, she said to herself, each jostling to be the first; captive little creatures which, this morning, were almost hostile.

She knew why. On returning home the previous day, she'd phoned the agency to say she didn't feel well—no, no, nothing serious, must be something she'd eaten, she'd be fine after a day's rest—and had stuffed the books unceremoniously into a big shopping bag and zipped it shut, then plonked the bag by the front door, with her umbrella on top of it because rain had been forecast. Then she'd switched on the TV, turned up the volume, and eaten frozen lasagne heated up in the microwave while she watched a documentary on gannets, then another about a has-been rock star. She needed the noises of the world as a buffer between her and the book depot, between her and the time she'd just spent in that tiny room—no, not tiny but cramped, that office where the remaining empty space seemed to have been carved out from the inside by each book arranged on a shelf or stacked between the legs of a table, against an armchair or on the shelves of an old refrigerator with its door open.

What she had brought back from that room, she'd removed from her sight, from her senses, if not from her memory; her mouth full of the almost sweet taste of industrial lasagne, her eardrums ringing with music, exclamations, birdcalls, secrets, analyses, chatter, she regained her footing in the familiar, the everyday, the not-too-bad, the almost bearable—in other words, life—the only life she knew.

And now, the books seemed to bear her a grudge for having ignored them. That was nonsense.

"Hey," complained the man next to her, a short, pudgy man in a camouflage parka, "your bag's rock hard. What the hell have you got in there?"

Looking at the top of his shiny, balding head, she replied automatically: "Books."

"At your age? I don't believe it. Not that I'm against books, but you'd do better to—"

Juliette didn't hear the rest of his sentence because the train shuddered to a halt, the doors opened, and the belligerent man, swept along by the tide of bodies, was already out of sight. A tall, slim woman with a creased raincoat took his place. She did not complain, even though for the entire duration of the journey she bounced against the books, which seemed to have arranged themselves to stab her as hard as possible at the slightest contact. Juliette felt bad for her and pressed herself against the juddering partition, but the woman's face, which she glimpsed in profile, did not betray the slightest annoyance; only a heavy weariness, like a thick shell, encrusted and hardened by time.

At last, she reached her station, wove her way through the stream of commuters going up and down the stairs, stumbled as she stepped onto the pavement, made a beeline for the agency, the sea of property ads—white rectangles with a bright orange border—and ran to the door.

She was the first in, so she was able to dump the bag under her jacket in the metal cupboard where the staff kept their personal belongings. Then she slammed the door with needless force and sat down at her desk, where a pile of incomplete files was waiting for her, plus a Post-it note covered in Chloe's untidy scrawl:

U feeling better? Doing a viewing now, then on to that awful flat in Rue G. XXX!

"That awful flat in Rue G" meant a very, very long viewing. The fifty-square-meter apartment was almost entirely taken up by a passageway and a disproportionately spacious bathroom containing a claw-foot bathtub eaten away by rust. Chloe had made this her personal challenge. A few days earlier, Juliette had listened to her drawing up her battle plan, enumerating enthusiastically the benefits of such a bathtub bang in the middle of Paris.

"If it's a couple, it'll enhance their sex life. They simply have to imagine themselves in it, with loads of foam and perfumed oil for foot massages."

"What about the rust, and the cracked linoleum? I don't find that very glamorous," Juliette had objected.

"I'm going to take my grandmother's antique Chinese rug over there—it's in the basement, my mother won't even notice it's gone—and a potted plant. They'll think they're in a conservatory, you see, like in that book you lent me. It's a pain, and it's very long—I couldn't get to the end of it—but there was that cool thing, full of flowers, with wicker chairs . . ."

Yes, Juliette knew exactly what she meant. The book was Zola's *The Kill*, which Chloe had returned to her, saying: "They make so much fuss about nothing!" But she had apparently enjoyed the seduction scene in the conservatory, when Renée Saccard gives herself to her young stepson amid the heady fragrances of the rare blooms, boasting of her husband's fortune and good taste.

"You should have come to the home-staging training event," Chloe chastised her. "It was amazing. You've got to put life into the properties—the life people crave. You want them to say, as they walk in, 'If I live here, I'll be stronger, more successful, more popular. I'll get that promotion I've been after for two years and that I haven't dared ask for because I'm scared of having the door slammed in my face. I'll earn five hundred euros a month more. I'll ask out that girl in the advertising department and she'll say yes.'"

"You're selling them an illusion . . ."

"No, a dream. And I help them imagine themselves in a better future," concluded Chloe solemnly.

The phone rang. It was Chloe: "Bring me a book. You've got loads in your desk drawer. I've seen them," she said accusingly.

"What kind of book?" asked Juliette, slightly disconcerted. "And why do—?"

"Any book. It's for the little table I'm going to put next to the bathtub. It'll hide the rust. I'm also going to put a vintage lamp with a bead fringe on it. Apparently, some girls love reading in the bath. You immediately feel the ambience."

"I thought you wanted to suggest erotic games in the bath?"

"Her guy isn't always there. And anyway, it's good to chill occasionally."

"If you say so," replied Juliette, amused. Chloe was into one-night stands, bemoaned every weekend spent without a lover as if it were a tragedy, and would certainly never have thought of inviting Proust or Faulkner to join her in a bubble bath.

"I'll see what I can do," she said before hanging up.

Chloe had been right: Juliette's bottom desk drawer, the deepest, which made it impractical for keeping files in order, was stuffed with paperbacks, the vestiges of four years of commuting, books between whose pages she had slipped bookmarks—cinema tickets or dry-cleaning receipts, a pizzeria flyer, concert programs, or pages torn from a notebook on which she'd scribbled shopping lists or telephone numbers.

When she yanked the metal handle, the heavy drawer slid along its runners with a grating sound then jammed, and half a dozen books tumbled to the floor. Juliette retrieved them and sat up to place them next to her keyboard. No point rummaging through the drawer; the first title that came to hand would do.

"Title" being the key word here, as that was all Chloe would read.

The title. Yes, it was important. Would people read Lorette Nobécourt's novel about psoriasis, *The Itching*, in the bath? Her skin still remembered that book: just holding it caused a furtive prickling, starting from her left shoulder blade and making its way up to her neck, and there she was scratching, even clawing herself. No, that wasn't a good idea. And yet, once she'd started reading it, she couldn't put it down. But then the bathwater was likely to go cold. What was needed was gentleness, something comforting, enveloping. And mysterious. Short stories? Maupassant's "The Horla," the unfinished journal of a descent into madness leading to suicide? Juliette pictured the reader, up to her neck in foam, looking up, gazing anxiously through the half-open door into the dark passage . . .

From the shadows, her childhood ghosts and fears so carefully repressed over the years would appear with their attendant anxieties . . . The young woman would sit up, panic-stricken, clamber out of the bath, skid on the soap like Lady Cora Crawley in Downton Abbey, possibly breaking her neck as she fell . . .

No.

She also discarded with regret the first volume of Proust's *In Search of Lost Time*, several thrillers with tattered covers, an essay on work-related suffering, a biography of Stalin (why had she bought that?), a French–Spanish conversation handbook, two fat Russian novels in ten-point, single-spaced type (unreadable), and sighed. Selecting the right book wasn't so straightforward after all.

She'd have to empty the drawer. There was bound to be something suitable in there. An inoffensive book, incapable of triggering even the slightest disaster.

Unless . . .

With the palm of her hand, Juliette swept the books haphazardly into the tomblike drawer, then closed it. It was sad, she could feel it, but for now she didn't want to dwell on this vague and unpleasant emotion.

She had a mission to carry out.

She stood up, walked around the desk, and opened the cupboard.

The bag was still there. Why had she fleetingly thought it

might have vanished? She leaned over, picked it up, and instinctively hugged it to her.

The corner of a book poked her between the ribs.

This is the one, she thought, with a certainty she had never felt before.

7

It was the first, her first as a book *passeur*, thought Juliette, feeling the chosen book through the thick fabric of her bag—but had she chosen it? She was already breaking the rules: she didn't even know the title of the book, didn't know whose hand would pick it up and turn it over, perhaps to read the back-cover blurb; she had neither followed nor observed her target, hadn't planned the moment when they'd meet, or matched the book and its reader with the care that Soliman had insisted was essential.

A female reader. It would be a woman, no question. Men don't read in the bath. Besides, men don't take baths; they're always in a hurry, and the only way to get them to sit still is to plonk them down on a sofa in front of the Champions League semifinal.

At least that was what Juliette had gleaned from the behavior of her previous three boyfriends.

"I know," she said out loud. "I'm making generalizations. That's why I screw up every time."

She was making generalizations again. But she had to admit that she tended to jump to hasty conclusions, usually optimistic, from the smallest detail that she found attractive: this one's little steel-rimmed spectacles, that one's arms held out, hands cupped to hold a puppy or a baby, and the third one's lock of hair that kept tumbling across his forehead and obscuring his intense blue gaze. In those tiny details, she thought she read intelligence, kindness, humor, dependability, or a power of imagination that she believed she herself lacked.

She plunged her hand into the bag with a frown, still talking to herself: Joseph had broad shoulders beneath the chunky knit sweaters he liked to wear, but his strength was limited to his ability to crush a walnut in his fist; Emmanuel felt sorry for the birds that flew into high-voltage cables but didn't call when she had the flu; Romain couldn't bear being teased even gently, and when they ate out he split the bill down to the last cent.

She had been in love—or thought she had, which boiled down to the same thing—with each of them. For the past six months, she'd been single. She had also thought she wouldn't be able to cope, and was surprised now at how much she was enjoying her freedom—the freedom that had so frightened her before.

"They can all get lost," she grumbled, closing her fingers around the chosen book—no, the book that had in fact forced itself on her.

The book was fat, dense; it fitted nicely into her hand. That was a plus. Juliette slowly retreated, her eyes glued to the near-black cover, with a glimpse, on the spine, of the hazy ruins of an English manor house.

Daphne du Maurier. *Rebecca.*

"They've put in an offer!"

Chloe flung her bag onto her desk, turned to Juliette, and pointed a mock accusing finger at her. "The girl made a bee-line for your book. Luckily, because she was looking a bit pissed off. I won't bore you with what she said about the living room, or the kitchen. But then, suddenly . . ."

She mimed wonderment, raising her eyebrows, her eyes wide and her mouth making an *O.*

"You get the picture. She goes into the bathroom—I must say I pulled out all the stops: soft lighting, the plant, a white bath sheet draped over the back of the chaise longue, you couldn't see the rust or the damp patches or anything. He started saying that it was mad, all the wasted space, but she wasn't even listening to him. She went over to the bath and then"—Chloe was jumping up and down, her fists clenched, and went on excitedly—"I've never seen anything like it! She picks up the book, begins to leaf through it, and says: 'Oh, *Rebecca,* my mother used to love that old film with . . . now who was it? Grace Kelly? No, Joan Fontaine.' And she starts reading. She can't put it down. I didn't even dare breathe. He says: 'I think we've seen enough,' and she goes: 'We could have a walk-in wardrobe,' and smiles. And I promise you, she asks me: 'Is this your book? Can I keep it?' And she plops herself in front of the mirror, a gorgeous baroque mirror I found in a thrift store last weekend, she fusses with her hair, like this"—Chloe mimed the girl's movements, and Juliette saw her eyelashes flutter, her face soften, become transformed, haunted by a sadness that was unlike her, that seemed to have been plastered over her laughing features like a Japanese Noh or a carnival mask—"and she turned to him and said in a strange voice: 'We'll be happy here . . . you'll see.'"

The estate agency closed at 6:30 P.M. At midnight, Juliette was still sitting on the wooden floorboards, which had long since lost their varnish and were worn down to wide, putty-colored stripes. Refurbishing this office, where clients never came— the girls had a Perspex table in the shop, which they took turns sitting at during the day, smiling affably under the glare of the recessed lighting—had been utterly out of the question since the New Year's party three years earlier, when Monsieur Bernard had knocked over a bottle of premium dry cider in the narrow passage leading to the window. The sparkling liquid had run into the cracks in the floor, leaving a yellowish aureole. It was on that stain, long since dried out, that Juliette was sitting cross-legged, the books arranged in a fan around her.

Seventeen books. She'd counted them. Held them, sized them up, flicked through them. She'd inhaled the smell of their folds, peeked at the odd sentence, words as appetizing as sweets, or sharp as blades: *With this he leapt up and made a bed for Odysseus nearer the fire, throwing sheep and goatskins over it. Then Odysseus lay down again, and the swineherd covered him with a big thick blanket, that he kept there for a dry covering after a fierce storm . . . My face was a meadow grazed by a herd of buffalo . . . He looked at the fire of logs, with its one flame pirouetting on the top in a dying dance after the breakfast-cooking and boiling . . . It is discovered. What? Eternity. In the whirling light of sun become sea . . . Yes, thought Rudy, ambitious men with powerful legs planted firmly on the ground, without the least gracious bending of the knee . . . Dinner jacket, vast dusks, the thirst for time, a meager moonlight, verbiage, dell, light . . .*

So many words. So many stories, characters, landscapes, laughter, tears, sudden decisions, hopes, and fears.

But for whom?

Juliette was back on the same street, with the rusty gate striped with old blue paint and the sky enclosed by high walls, and she was surprised. It would have felt perfectly natural if the road had vanished and she'd found herself facing a blank wall, or if she'd searched in vain for the book depot, only to discover it had been replaced by a pharmacy or a supermarket with fluorescent yellow or green boards advertising the week's special offers.

No. She placed the flat of her left hand on the cold metal. The nameplate, too, was still there. And the bookstop, allowing a smoky draft to escape through the double door. She turned around and stared at the facades across the street. Why was she suddenly worried about being watched? Was she afraid that someone might see her going in and judge her? In this sleepy neighborhood, people probably watched their neighbors' comings and goings with suspicion. And this place was bound to arouse their curiosity, if not more. Juliette didn't know what she was afraid of. But she felt the stirrings of a vague anxiety. Giving books to strangers—strangers you hand-picked and spied on—who would devote time to that? Devote all their time, even? What did the father and little Zaide live on? Did he sometimes go out to work despite what he'd said? The thought brought no image to mind, and Juliette couldn't imagine Soliman behind a bank window or at an architecture firm, even less in a classroom or at a supermarket checkout. Or did he stay shut away, far removed from day and night, in that book-lined room with the lights on all day long? He might very well work there, designing websites, doing translations, writing freelance articles or catalog copy, for example. But she couldn't picture him in any of those roles. The fact was that she couldn't see him as a real person, an ordinary person with material needs and a social life; nor could she see him as a father.

Nor really as a man.

We are taught to be suspicious, she thought, as she pushed the heavy door, which opened slowly, almost reluctantly. *Always to expect the worst. Giving books to people, to make them feel better—if I've understood correctly . . . I'm sure the woman in the corner grocery shop thinks Soliman's a terrorist or a drug dealer. And that the police have already been here. If he were a dentist, that thought wouldn't cross anyone's mind.*

The courtyard was deserted. A scrap of paper was fluttering on the bottom steps of the metal staircase, and the office door was closed. No light inside. Disappointed but reluctant to leave, Juliette made her way over to the grimy windows, spurred on by curiosity. The beast's lair without the beast— the thrill of danger without the danger. Why was she making these strange comparisons?

Why not, though? She edged toward the window. The silence was extraordinary. Impossible, or almost, to believe that a few meters away rumbled the city, devourer of time, of flesh, of dreams, the city never sated, never sleeping. A flapping of wings signaled to her that a pigeon had landed on the guard-rail of the gallery above her head; a cracked bell could be heard striking eight. Morning. It could have been any hour, anywhere, in one of those country towns that Balzac was fond of describing.

"Don't stand there. Come in."

The voice came from up above. It floated toward her, making her jump. She hadn't glued her nose to the window, but still she felt as if she'd been caught red-handed snooping.

"I'm coming. I'm a bit late today."

He was already there—as if he'd moved without touching the ground. Juliette hadn't even heard his footsteps on the stairs. Before he appeared, she caught a whiff of the fragrance that permeated his clothes, a blend of cinnamon and orange.

"I've just made a cake for Zaide," he said. "She's a bit under the weather."

He looked at his hands, covered in flour, and wiped them on his black trousers with an apologetic smile.

He was a hands-on father after all. But a cake? For a little girl who was unwell?

"If she's got a tummy ache . . ." Juliette began disapprovingly, before biting her tongue, because she suddenly heard her mother's and her grandmother's voices coming out of her own mouth.

What business was it of hers, for goodness' sake?

Soliman pulled down the handle but the door's rusty hinges resisted. He forced it open with one shove of his shoulder.

"Everything's askew here," he said. "The walls and their occupant. We go well together."

Juliette should have protested—out of politeness—but actually he was right. She smiled. *Askew* . . . the word had a certain charm. As did the stone doorstep with its grooves forming parallel curves, the floor gray with dust, the windows whose panes trembled at the slightest breath of wind, the ceiling lost in the semidarkness, and the books piled up in every nook and cranny. And yet the overall effect of this haphazardly created place was one of solidity; this place that could have vanished overnight, like a mirage, could have been transported in its entirety through time and space to reappear elsewhere, without the door ceasing to creak or the piles of books collapsing as visitors walked past. You could come to like the soft, muffled thud, the rustle of crumpled pages; but Soliman rushed over and, indicating a free chair, gathered, consolidated, and pushed away the scaffoldings of books with concerned kindness.

"Have you already finished?" he asked at last, breathless, as he sat down. "Tell me."

"Oh! No. That's not it. I . . ." But he wasn't listening.

"Tell me," he urged. "Maybe I forgot to explain: I write everything down."

He placed the palm of his hand on a big, green, dog-eared register. Juliette, who could once more feel herself slipping into—into what? Another country, another time, perhaps— became absorbed in contemplating that hand. It was a large hand, the fingers widely spaced, covered in brown downy hair. Trembling. Like a little animal. Short nails, edged not with black but with dull gray, the gray of dust, book dust, of course. Ink returned to powder, words returned to ash and accumulated here, therefore able to escape, fly, be inhaled, and perhaps understood.

"Everything?"

This time, her voice expressed neither surprise nor wariness; rather . . . perhaps . . . a childlike wonder. No. That word, *wonder*, was mawkish, or strong, too strong. Too strong for suspicion, irony, indifference. Too strong for everyday life.

I'm going to get up, decided Juliette, dazed. *I'm going to leave and never come back. I'll go to the cinema, why not, and then eat sushi, or a pizza, and I'll go home and I'll . . .*

You'll do what, Juliette? You'll sleep? You'll flop down and watch a stupid program on TV? Wallow once again in your solitude?

"Yes, everything. Everything that people tell me. The history of the books. The way they live, the people they touch—each book is a portrait and it has at least two faces."

"Two . . ."

"Yes. The face of the person who gives it, and the face of the person who receives it."

Soliman's hand rose and hovered briefly over a pile that was not as high as the others.

"These ones here, for example. Someone brought them to me. That doesn't happen often. I don't write my address on the flyleaves. I like knowing that they get lost, that they follow paths unknown to me . . . after their first passage through my hands, of which I preserve a trace, an account."

He took the book from the top of the pile without opening it. His fingers slid along the fore edge. A caress. Juliette couldn't help shivering.

He's not even good-looking.

"It was the woman I told you about the other day, the one you met on the Métro, who passed on this book. And then I found it wedged in the door yesterday. I don't know who left it there. And that makes me sad."

Buffeted by the east wind, a strong wind that had been blowing on and off since the previous day, the train swayed gently
and, when she closed her eyes, Juliette imagined herself aboard
a ship setting sail, leaving the calm, smooth waters of a port
for the open seas.

She needed this image to calm herself down, to quell her
shaking hands. The book she was holding open in front of her
felt stiff, much too thick, too conspicuous, to be honest.

But wasn't this what she wanted?

The cardboard cover kept slipping. She had made it the day
before, helping herself from the office stationery cupboard,
using and abusing the color printer to the point where they'd
probably have to change the cartridges twice this month—
an expense that Monsieur Bernard would frown upon. She'd
thrown the botched attempts into the wastepaper basket, then
changed her mind and stuffed them into a big bin bag, which
she'd dumped in a trash can three streets away, with a vague
feeling of guilt. Once again, she marked the fold of the flaps

and wedged the book on her knees. Opposite her, a guy in his thirties, fitted suit and thin tie straight out of the sixties, stopped bashing away on his smartphone to give her a rather emphatic look of commiseration, she thought.

Juliette covertly observed the other occupants of the compartment. There weren't many people. Public-sector workers were on strike; reduced service on the suburban express trains. The commuters had stayed home—those who could, at least. And, for once, she was early, very early even. It was barely 7:30. Why had she chosen this early-morning hour? Oh yes: she was afraid of not getting a seat. The book she was reading, or pretending to read, was not the kind you could hold in one hand while hanging on to one of the straps by the doors with the other.

So none of her habitual traveling companions were to be seen. She felt almost relieved.

No one was taking any notice of her, except the guy with the smartphone. He was leaning forward, his chin jutting out, his eyebrows raised in an exaggerated expression of amazement.

"Are you really going to read all that?" He let out a shrill laugh, leaned a little closer, and tapped the book jacket with his nail. "It's a joke."

Juliette merely shook her head. No, it wasn't a joke. But she hadn't found a better way of snaring her potential prey. She didn't feel capable of deducing from a person's appearance their character, their tastes, and their dreams, or of choosing a suitable nourishment for those dreams. That is what she had explained to Soliman the other day, after their argument.

Argument was perhaps a little strong. Can you talk about an "argument" when you're fumbling around in your bag—under the hairbrush, the book begun ages ago, the keys, those of the agency, those of the basement of her building, the mobile phone, a notebook full of scribbles and never-ending to-do lists—looking for a slightly crumpled but clean tissue for a man sobbing uncontrollably?

No, Juliette corrected herself. *Now you're writing the novel and you're overdoing it.*

Rewind.

She had told him everything, as he had demanded: the passage with a bend and the bathroom, dark, damp, and ridiculously big compared to the other rooms in the apartment, the claw-foot bathtub, the rust stains, Chloe's ideas and her home-staging training, the indoor plant, the draped bath sheet, and finally the book. And the unhoped-for success: the clients had already signed the sale commitment, they didn't need a mortgage—cash buyers—they'd already booked a contractor, and they seemed over the moon.

And Soliman, who had listened to her attentively but without taking any notes, had dried, almost without thinking, a glistening tear on his cheek—which she would not have seen had it not been for the glaring light from the lamp whose shade was raised.

But she couldn't have failed to notice the one that followed.

And other tears had taken the same path; gentle, slow, rolling down his cheeks and being transformed on contact with a two-day stubble into a thin film, which he no longer attempted to wipe away.

"I don't understand," whispered Juliette. "Is something the matter? I . . ."

Yes, of course something was the matter. She'd done everything wrong—as usual.

Then she'd tipped out the contents of her bag onto the desk, hunting for a packet of tissues, and eventually found one, which she offered him.

"I'm sorry, truly sorry."

She couldn't think of any better word.

"Sorry, sorry," she repeated.

"Stop."

"Sor—You don't understand, I'm not clever like that woman, the one who killed herself. Or like the others, your *passeurs*. I don't know them, I don't know. I'm incapable of guessing someone's character just from watching them during a Métro journey. And I can't follow people around all day, otherwise I'll lose my job. So how can I know what book they need?"

He blew his nose vigorously.

"That's a stupid thing to say," he croaked.

"But you can see . . ."

And then they'd begun to laugh hysterically, a contagious, irrepressible laughter. Bent double, her hands pressed between her knees, Juliette laughed until she cried. Soliman was clutching the lampstand with both hands and hiccupping, which made the lampshade tip up and bathe his face in green shadow.

"You . . . you . . . look like . . . a zombie . . ." Juliette had managed to stammer before stamping her feet, her leg muscles twitching madly.

How good it was to laugh like that, mouth wide open, without worrying about making an idiot of herself for once. To scream with laughter, hiccup, wipe off the saliva drooling down her chin, and start all over again.

They were still laughing when Zaide burst into the office, closing the door very carefully behind her and then turning around and staring at them with a solemn expression.

She was hugging a book—and her hands, noticed Juliette, who'd stopped laughing abruptly, were like finer replicas of her father's. The same attentive care to ensure she held the book firmly by the spine, the same delicacy. Each of her pink, almost pearly nails was a little masterpiece.

But that was not what had held Juliette's attention.

Zaide's book was encased in thick, slightly undulating cardboard, a bright green, on which thin red felt letters had been carefully glued—even if they were slightly wonky.

And those letters said:

This book is amazing.
It will make you clever.
It will make you happy.

10

"It's a joke," repeated the guy in the too-tight suit. Juliette looked up at his laughing face and—thinking of Zaide and trying to imitate the expression of attentive solemnity that she'd caught on the little girl's features—retorted: "No, not at all."

"You're . . . you're a member of a . . . a group, I mean a kind of sect, is that it?"

The word sent a slight shiver down Juliette's spine, as if a feather with prickly barbs had brushed her, barely touching but enough to alert her.

A sect. Wasn't that what she'd thought when she'd come back from the depot? Perhaps even the first time she'd set foot inside? A sect, a sort of prison without bars or locks, something that clung to your skin, wormed its way inside you, obtained your consent, not even forced, no, on the contrary, it was given with relief, with enthusiasm, with the sense of having found a family at last, a purpose, something solid, that would neither crumble nor disappear; clear, simple certainties—like the words Zaide had cut out, one letter at a time, then glued onto the cover of her book, or rather, her books, all the ones she loved, she'd explained.

"Because it's complicated explaining why you love a book. And I can't always do it. There are books that when I've read them I feel . . . well . . . something stirs inside me. But I can't show it. So, now I've said it and people should just try them."

She had shot her father a slightly disdainful look.

"Me, I don't run after anyone. But then there are some people who don't budge at all."

Soliman had held out his hand across the desk.

"I know what you mean, darling."

His voice was very calm, and his right eyelid had a twitch, a tiny quiver. Zaide had blushed, and Juliette couldn't help admiring the sight, that slow infusion of blood beneath her olive skin, from her neck to her cheekbones and to the corners of her eyes, which had filled with tears.

"I'm sorry, Papa. I'm a naughty girl. A naughty girl!"

And she turned on her heel and fled, her head bowed, hugging the book to her.

"No," replied Juliette with a firmness that surprised even her, "I don't belong to a sect. I love books, that's all."

She could have added: *I don't always like people.* That was what she was thinking, at that moment, looking at him. His grin showing yellowish incisors, gap teeth, that old-fashioned healthy look, fat, pink, self-satisfied, slightly condescending.

Chloe would have labeled him immediately: *That guy's a pig, forget it.*

"Do you want it?" she went on.

Suspicion at once took the place of the assured smile on the man's chubby face.

"Oh no, I'm not interested. I haven't got any change and—"

"I don't want to sell it to you. I'm giving it to you."

"You mean it's free?"

He looked gobsmacked. And suddenly greedy. He nervously ran his tongue over his fat lips, looked right and left, and leaned toward her again. The smell of aftershave engulfed Juliette, who held her breath.

"A catch," he suddenly decided, clenching his fists on his thighs. "There's always a catch with these freebies. You're going to ask me for my email address and I'll get spam till the end of the century."

"You'll be dead at the end of the century," Juliette pointed out softly. "And I don't want your email address. I'm giving you the book. I'll be getting off at the next stop and you can forget me."

She shut the book and placed it on her spread palms, which she raised toward him.

"Nothing in exchange. Free," she repeated, enunciating each syllable as if speaking to a child.

He looked taken aback. Almost frightened. Finally, he held out both hands and took the book. Cool air ran through Juliette's palms as the train drew into the station.

"Goodbye."

He didn't reply. She stood up, slipped the strap of her bag over her shoulder, and headed for the door behind a woman carrying her baby tied to her front with a long shawl. Over the woman's shoulder, two tiny black eyes stared at Juliette, peeping out from beneath a woolen hat with three pom-poms, one red, one yellow, and one purple.

"Peekaboo!" said Juliette, feeling emotional.

Other people's children always made her feel emotional, but the mothers terrified her—too confident, too competent, the opposite of what she felt she was.

The little nose wrinkled, the eyelids fluttered a fraction. That gaze. How could anyone stand that all day long, that perpetual questioning? Why? Why? Why? That tireless curiosity. Those open eyes like hungry mouths.

And that anger, at having been brought into this world, perhaps. This world.

On the platform, she took a few steps and then turned around. The guy was still staring at the closed book. He'd placed a palm down on the cover. Was he afraid it might open of its own accord? That monsters or mythological creatures would escape from it, something very ancient, dangerous, burning hot? Or too new to be confronted yet?

Juliette saw him go past as the train moved off, still hunched over, sitting motionless. His profile. His thick neck, with traces of the hair clippers. A man.

A reader?

11

"Are you going to tell me what you're up to?"

Chloe was standing in front of Juliette's desk, her arms folded. Her entire attitude announced that she wouldn't move until she'd been given an explanation.

"What are you talking about?"

A pathetic ploy to gain time—Juliette knew it. A few seconds. Not even, because her colleague was off again: "With those wretched books you're cramming into your drawer. With all the bits of torn cardboard I keep finding in the wastepaper baskets."

Again, Juliette sidestepped the question: "I thought they were emptied every evening . . ."

With a sharp swipe, the side of her hand cutting through the air, Chloe made it clear that that wasn't the issue.

"I'm waiting."

And, since Juliette still refused to say anything, she snapped: "You want to make more sales than me, is that it? You've perfected the trick?"

"What trick?" asked Juliette, who knew very well what Chloe was talking about.

"The home staging. The trick with the book on the side of the bath. Let me remind you that was my idea. You're not allowed to use it."

She was unrecognizable, her nostrils pinched, pale, with two bright stains on her cheekbones as if she'd hastily applied a blusher in the dark. Her fingers dug into the flabby flesh on her arms, her carefully manicured nails making little prawn-colored half-moons. Juliette stared at her as if she were a stranger, her mask of prettiness suddenly obliterated by anxiety and resentment, and thought she glimpsed her as she would be in thirty years' time, her features indelibly furrowed with bitterness and worry. Ugly. Gloomy.

Pathetic.

"Oh, Chloe!"

She felt like crying. Like getting up and putting her arms around her, cradling her, to cleanse her of a sorrow about which she knew nothing—and which Chloe probably didn't understand either.

"You've been warned."

Chloe turned on her heel and marched over to her desk, toward the garlands of Post-its stuck to the base of her desk light, toward her computer screen with its pink rabbit ears—a present from a customer who had designs on her, she claimed when she put them on, new and stiff, candy-floss pink. The pink had lost its color; the fabric was dusty now, and the fluffy ears had flopped down over the screen like faded iris leaves, projecting a long shadow.

Chloe marched like a frontline soldier in a 1950s war film, thought Juliette, with great strides and a forced determination, a spirit invigorated by danger and the prospect of failure. She believed in a purely imaginary rivalry, saw it as a battle that she had to win at all costs.

Juliette looked down at the file open in front of her, a lump in her throat. For some time, she'd had the feeling that life was passing her by, eluding her, thousands of grains of sand running through an almost invisible crack, taking with them thousands of images, colors, smells, scratches, and caresses, a hundred tiny disappointments and perhaps as many consolations . . . The fact was, she'd never liked her life very much, progressing from a boring childhood to a sullen adolescence before discovering at the age of nineteen, in the gazes she attracted, that she was beautiful—maybe. Some days. That there was inside her, as her first lover had whispered to her one night when they'd both had a little too much to drink, a gracefulness, something dancing, ethereal, something that allowed you to believe in the lightness of time, outside the dramas and the increasing misery of present-day reality.

But Juliette didn't feel equal to taking on that persona. She had proved it by leaving Gabriel, who had carried on alone, drinking too much and going from bar to bar seeking a woman, or rather, a myth, whose otherworldly virtues would make his life bearable. She had proved it by collecting the depressed, the aggressive, the bad-tempered, and the indecisive. She had sought, then fled, those willing victims; she had watched them wallowing in their despair in the same way she watched the spiders she drowned, reluctantly, in her shower.

Dancing, ethereal—her? Well, maybe in the way that ballerinas were, twirling on their tortured feet, their toes bleeding, a smile on their lips? And she found even that comparison smug: all those first-world problems, as she sometimes said to herself, comparing her limited but comfortable life to the real distress she glimpsed only fleetingly on TV.

But then, she reminded herself, there were also the little joys. Those of routine: when the coffee was good in the morning; when the rain forecasted for the week only fell at night. When the TV news wasn't a litany of deaths and atrocities, when she managed to remove from her favorite blouse the red pesto stain that Chloe had told her would never come out, when the latest Woody Allen film was really good . . .

And then there were books. Crammed into two rows on the living-room bookcase, in piles on either side of the bed, beneath the legs of the two little tables inherited from her grandmother, the firefly grandmother, the one who had lived her entire life in a little village clinging to the mountainside, in a house whose walls were as black as frozen lava; books in the bathroom cabinet, too, between the toiletries and the spare toilet paper; books on a shelf in the toilet and in a huge laundry basket whose handles had broken ages ago; books in the kitchen, next to the single pile of plates; a column of books in the hallway behind the coatrack. Juliette passively watched the gradual invasion of her space. She didn't put up a fight, simply moved a few volumes to her desk drawer when she'd tripped three times over the same one that had fallen from its pile or shelf, which meant, to her mind, that the book wanted to leave her, or at least, that it had taken a dislike to the apartment.

On Sundays, Juliette went to every garage sale because she ached at the sight of those boxes where old books had been chucked carelessly, almost with disdain, and which no one bought. People came for secondhand clothes, seventies bric-a-brac, and household appliances that were still in working order. They hadn't the slightest interest in books. So she bought them, filled her shopping basket with odd books, recipe or DIY books, sexy crime fiction, which she didn't like, just to hold them in her hand, give them a little TLC.

One day she'd gone into a tiny secondhand bookshop, sandwiched between a pharmacy and a church, in a square in Brussels. It was a dreary, wet weekend, and the tourists were staying away from the city after the terrorist attacks. She had been almost the only visitor at the Royal Museums of Fine Arts, where a superb collection of Flemish Old Masters slumbered beneath high glass roofs from which a wan light fell. Afterward she'd felt the need to warm herself up. She'd walked past several cafés, fantasizing about a hot chocolate, and then she'd found herself in front of three steps, worn down in the center from use. What had attracted her had been a box of books on sale outside, sitting on a garden chair under a huge red umbrella tied to the back of it. But the books were all in Flemish. She'd gone up the steps, jerked the old-fashioned handle, and opened the door. She found herself on familiar ground, among the piles of books, the paper dust, the smell of old bindings. At the back of the shop, a man sitting at a small table had barely looked up from the book he was reading when the little bell had jingled. Juliette wandered among the shelves for a long time, leafed through a nineteenth-century medical treatise, a home economics manual, a method for learning Latin like a living language, several old novels by Paul Bourget, an author who seemed vehemently opposed to divorce, an album on the butterflies of Brazil and, finally, a slim volume with a white cover, entitled *Vertical Poetry, Thirteenth Volume*, the bilingual edition. *Vertical—I wonder why,* she'd thought as she'd opened it. *Aren't the lines of the poems horizontal like in any other poetry book? Yes, but the layout . . . you could say that . . .*

The poet was called Roberto Juarroz. The collection had fallen open at page 81, and on page 81 she read:

We have not been taught
. . . to sustain ourselves on a shadow.

Juliette read and reread the poem, oblivious of the time. She stood rooted to the spot, the open book in her hands, while outside the drizzle turned into a downpour and rain lashed the glass door, making it shake and shudder. At the back of the shop, the bookseller was merely a hunched, silent shadow, his back covered with grayish dust. Perhaps he hadn't moved for centuries, since the establishment had been built, in 1758 according to the carved inscription on its stone pediment, so white against the dark red brickwork.

At last, he said, "Your umbrella."

Juliette jumped. "My umbrella?"

"It's dripping on the books in the box by your feet and making them wet. Put it by the door—it will be more convenient for you."

It was more of an invitation than a reprimand, but she closed the book and went over to him, a little too hastily.

"I'll take it," she mumbled, holding out the anthology.

"Juarroz."

He took the book in both hands and raised the spine to his face, closing his eyes and smiling, like a sommelier inhaling a great vintage just uncorked.

"Dear old Juarroz . . ."

He slid his thumb inside the book, moving it slowly up to the top of the page, a gesture in which the disconcerted Juliette saw sensuality and even love; then he pinched the page between two fingers, turning it with the same careful slowness, while his lips moved. At last, he looked up, offering Juliette, for the first time, the gaze of his gentle eyes, huge behind the pebble lenses of his glasses.

"I always find it a little painful to let go of them," he admitted. "I have to say goodbye . . . do you understand?"

"Yes," breathed Juliette.

"Take good care of it."

"I promise," she replied, gobsmacked.

On leaving the shop, she took three steps, then swung around abruptly and looked back at the shop front with the peeling paintwork enclosing its treasures. A gust of wind caught the red umbrella, bending it like a farewell wave.

A farewell wave. Juliette looked about her. The ill-lit office, the windows overlooking the back courtyard, gray with grime, the faded posters on the wall, and Chloe, who had just turned her screen so that her colleague couldn't see her expression; Chloe and her wild hair, her short, frilly skirts, her everyday cheeriness that rang so false. Chloe and her laugh that had just turned into a scowl. Chloe and her ambitions, Chloe and her calculations, Chloe and her profound, bitter inadequacy.

Behind Juliette was the wall of files, that toe-curlingly hideous urine-colored wall. And on the other side of the door, Monsieur Bernard, who sipped a hot drink from the cup that had been his mother's. Farther still, beyond the agency front, was the street, the cars driving past on the wet road with gentle squeals, more shops and hundreds, no thousands of boxes called *apartments*, which were bought and sold, and which contained thousands of strangers also ground down by ambitions, inhabited perhaps by blind rage; but also dreamers, lovers, blind mad folk who saw perhaps more clearly than others (where had she read that?). Yes, thousands and thousands of strangers existed out there, while she sat here, unmoving, surrounded by this constant tide. She was going to stay here, trying to calm Chloe's anger, knowing very well that she would never entirely succeed; she was going to stay here watching life go by, filling in forms and estimating the possible discount on the commission for a 140-square-meter apartment at Bir-Hakeim. She was going to stay here, and she was going to die.

Everyone was going to die. And she would never know them, never approach them, never speak to them, and all those stories walking past on the street inside the people carrying them—she would never know anything of them.

Without thinking, she slid out the left-hand drawer of her desk, the one where the books had been piling up since her arrival at the agency; one jammed in the groove and the drawer got stuck. She leaned over and took it by the corner to free it. Then she turned it over to read the title: *The End of Ordinary Times* by Florence Delay.

12

"You've handed in your notice."

Clasping his knee, Soliman rocked back and forth on his chair. When his knee banged against the table, he swung back again; the bookshelves behind him stopped him and sent him back toward Juliette, toward the subdued light of the lamp with the green shade, so the lower part of his face was alternately bathed in light or lost in the shadows again.

Juliette said nothing, because it was a statement rather than a question. She simply nodded, with a vigor that also seemed unnecessary.

"I gave them a book. Before leaving," she said.

"Only one?"

"No. One for Chloe, and one for Monsieur Bernard."

"Wait."

Two of the chair legs scraped across the floor noisily, and Soliman reached out to pick up his notebook, turning the pages with a strange frenzy.

"What day is it again? I ought to have a calendar here, a diary, I don't know . . ."

"Or a mobile phone," added Juliette, repressing a smile.

"I'd rather die."

He stopped short, frowned as if an unpleasant thought had just occurred to him, then shrugged.

"The thirteenth of January? No, the . . ."

"Fifteenth of February," Juliette corrected him.

"Already. How time flies. But I had a meeting yesterday at . . . it doesn't matter. Let's get back to work. Give me the address of your estate agency, the names of the readers, the approximate time . . . I always advise checking the time when you pass on a book, it's very important—"

"Why?"

He looked up from the notebook in which he had just drawn a horizontal line with a ruler. She noticed that he was paler than usual, and that there was a red streak under his cheekbone.

Maybe he'd cut himself shaving. Today, his black hair, disheveled as always, looked dull and lifeless.

"What do you mean, why?"

"You don't even know what day it is."

"Oh? You must be right . . ."

He kept quiet while she gave the information he'd asked for. He hadn't answered her question except by ignoring it, and a vague, inexplicable sadness made her shiver.

"As a matter of fact," he suddenly broke in, "the time . . . I don't know whether you'll understand, you're still a novice. But time . . . Do you pass on a book in the same way at six o'clock in the morning as you do at ten o'clock at night? I write all this down so that you—you and the others—can refer to this notebook at any time. That way, you'll remember. It will even be better than a memory, because the mention of the date and the time encompasses an infinite number of things: the season and the light, to mention only the most obvious. Were you wearing a heavy coat or a summer dress? What about the other person? How were they dressed? How did they move? Had the sun already set? Was it skimming the rooftops or flooding dark courtyards, the ones you can barely make out between stations? Was there not, in one of those courtyards, a woman at her window, no, a child, who waved as the train passed, as if wishing good luck to friends setting off on a long journey? If it was in December, you would only have been able to guess at the light of a lamp behind the windowpanes, perhaps the rapid swish of a curtain being drawn back and the pale smudge of a face . . ."

With those last words, Soliman's voice had dropped to a whisper. He was talking to himself, Juliette realized, evoking a particular memory. A memory she couldn't share, even though the scene seemed almost alive, more real than her own presence in that office. She always came back to the feeling that overwhelmed her as soon as she set foot in the room, the sense she was walking through a mirage—one of those beautiful shimmering images that desert caravans see from a distance, so she'd learned as a child, but which recede as the thirsty travelers approach. She, Juliette, had walked straight into that illusion and ever since had been battling at night against books rising up from their stacks and flying like birds in a courtyard enclosed by high walls, and tables without legs, and doors made of dense, colored fog; pages sometimes escaped from them and whirled around, flying so high that they fluttered out of sight . . .

"Juliette," said Soliman abruptly, "I'd like to ask you a favor."

She blinked, disconcerted. She had almost seen the books jump from the shelves, and was no longer certain she wasn't dreaming.

"Yes, yes, of course," she hurriedly replied. "If I can help you, it would be a pleasure. I have time, lots of time, now."

"I'm delighted. For selfish reasons."

He stood up and began to pace up and down the room, although "pace up and down" wasn't the right expression, Juliette thought; the space was so cluttered. It would be more accurate to say he walked sideways, crablike, taking two steps, going backward, brushing the cover of a book or placing his hand on it heavily. Perhaps that way the words passed through the cardboard or the leather; permeated his skin and nourished the scrawny body swaying slowly in the half-darkness.

"I'd like to know . . . whether you could . . . move in here."

Juliette stared at him openmouthed. He had his back to

her, but her silence must have alarmed him, and he swung round, waving his hands in denial.

"It's not what you think. Let me explain." And he executed a strange sidestep, which took him back to his table where he sat to one side, his arms folded.

"I have to go away. For . . . a while."

"Go away?" echoed Juliette. "Where?"

"It doesn't matter. What does matter is that I can't take Zaide. And that there's no one to take my place here. You are the only person I can ask to do this."

There was such anguish in his eyes that Juliette couldn't find the words to reply, even less the breath she felt sucked up, crushed by a revelation that was late in coming but the weight of which could already be felt, inside them, between them.

At last, she took a breath and was able to say: "Are you . . . all right?"

"I'll be fine. In a few months. I'm certain. But I want to spare my daughter any worry. She thinks I'm going on a journey, and that you're coming to live here to take care of her, that's all."

He raised a hand, palm toward Juliette, as if putting up a barrier. *No questions*, his eyes said.

No questions, Juliette silently assented.

"Under the gallery, next to our place, there are two free rooms. They need a lick of paint, but I've had a shower put in, hot plates . . . if it suits you . . . rent-free, of course. And I'll pay you for—"

"Can I see them first? And then . . . I'll need a little time to think. Let's say until tomorrow. That's it: I'll give you my answer tomorrow. That won't be too late for you?"

He smiled and stood up, visibly relieved.

"No, of course not. I'll see you out."

13

Three weeks later, Juliette moved into her new home. Daylight only entered the two rooms, both former workshops, from the gallery and a narrow skylight; until nightfall they were bathed in a uniform pale light which Juliette soon came to find restful. In one of the stockrooms, Soliman had unearthed some huge pots of daffodil-yellow paint, brushes so stiff that they had to be soaked for two whole days, and tarpaulins, which they spread on the floor before setting to work. Very soon, the stripped walls were covered with broad swathes of yellow, applied as they moved around, to the rhythm of their rambling conversations. Zaide crouched in the corner nearest the door, armed with the brush from her watercolor set and a palette where little blobs of gouache overlapped, ran into each other, and blended. She was painting flowers on the skirting—dark blue roses with red stems, green daisies with purple centers, black tulips "like the one Rosa grew in her room for poor Cornelius, the prisoner."

"She's engrossed in Alexandre Dumas, a real bookworm," Soliman explained with pride.

"No questions," recalled Juliette, who was dying to ask some. So they talked about colors, flowers, tulip fever, oriental gardens divided into four sections to reflect paradise. "Paradise," in fact, came from a Persian word, *pairidaeza*, explained Soliman, which meant "garden enclosure."

"I'd prefer a garden without walls," said Juliette, noticing that the old denim dungarees she'd put on that morning were as spattered with yellow as an entire field of buttercups.

"I like walls," stated Zaide without looking up. "They protect you."

"No one wants to hurt you, *ziba*," said Soliman softly.

"You have no idea, you don't. You have no idea what's on the other side of the wall because you never go out."

"But I had to get in, didn't I?"

"Yes," crooned Zaide, "you had to, you had to . . ."

They stopped there. Juliette would have loved to know how the father and daughter had landed here, what their journey had been, where they'd come from, from what garden or what war, perhaps. She couldn't help telling herself stories about them, and their floating, truncated, uncertain destinies added further to the charm surrounding them and this place that resembled a ship washed up on a beach, given over to a certain neglect and yet so alive.

They talked about books and more books, about the gothic novels of Horace Walpole and Joyce's *Dubliners*, about Italo

Calvino's fantastic tales, and the short, enigmatic prose of Robert Walser, or Sei Shōnagon's *The Pillow Book*, García Lorca's poetry, and that of the twelfth-century Persian poets. Soliman abandoned his paintbrush to recite lines by Nizami:

> On lofty Beysitoun the lingering sun
> Looks down on ceaseless labors, long begun;
> The mountain trembles to the echoing sound
> Of falling rocks that from her sides rebound.

> The hands of Peris might have wrought those stems
> Where dewdrops hang their fragile diadems

> "Alas! Shireen!" at every stroke he cries;
> At every stroke fresh miracles arise:
> "For thee these glories and these wonders all,
> For thee I triumph or for thee I fall;
> For thee my life one ceaseless toil has been,
> Inspire my soul anew—Alas! Shireen!"

And Juliette pressed her nose to the wall, churned up by those words, *but why churned up,* she wondered as she smoothed the contour of a doorframe. *I'm not in love with him and yet he's going away like Shireen, and all this, the depot, these rooms, his office, will seem empty, despite Zaide's voice, her singing, her games, and her toys, which I'll pick up from the steps of the fire escape, despite the* passeurs *and the books, despite—*

"Don't you like poetry?"

What an idiot. He'd completely misunderstood. And so had she, for that matter. It must be part of the inescapable human condition—each person ultimately deaf, impervious to other people's emotions, incapable of deciphering gestures, looks, or silences, all condemned to give painful explanations with words that are never the right ones.

"Yes . . . yes, I do like poetry. But the smell of paint is giving me a bit of a headache."

The lie was blatant, but he was completely taken in, offering her a chair, water, an aspirin, and finally suggesting she go and get some fresh air, which Juliette gratefully agreed to do. She went out into the gallery and walked up and down, watching the courtyard, the buildings framing it on three sides, which mostly showed only their windowless facades. No one could spy on what was happening there; it was a perfect refuge in the center of Paris—a refuge or an isolated, protected lair. And again, the old insidious suspicion surfaced. Had Soliman told her the truth? Were his self-imposed reclusiveness and seemingly harmless obsessions a cover for something else? Juliette didn't dare think what that "something else" might be, but despite her efforts to stifle them, images assailed her— bloody, atrocious images, which all the television channels had broadcast nonstop, and also those cordoned-off doorways with the doors smashed in, behind which you could glimpse a gutted interior, weapons—they'd found weapons and also lists, names, places. Neighbors were questioned. "He was so polite," said an old lady. "He'd hold the elevator door open for me and carry my shopping . . ."

Juliette wiped both hands over her face before realizing that her fingers were paint-stained—*I'm going to look like a dandelion*—and she laughed nervously in an attempt to banish the terrifying images, the fear, everything that was going to make her life impossible if she wasn't careful. *Come on, Juliette, terrorists don't recite poetry: they hate poetry, music, and everything that speaks of love.* It was another cliché, but she tried to cling to it. When you're drowning you don't choose your lifeline.

"Here, this will do you good." He was behind her, holding out a smoked-glass tumbler from which a thin wisp of steam rose. "It's spiced tea."

"Thank you," she murmured.

Ashamed, she plunged her nose into the fragrant mist, closed her eyes, and imagined herself far away, very far, at one of those Middle Eastern markets which the bombs had reduced to rubble in one of those gardens that no longer exist except in fairy tales. She took a sip.

"It's good," she said.

Soliman was leaning on the rusty iron rail, looking up at the sky, which was slowly turning mauve.

"Soon there won't be enough light to paint."

"We can always turn the lamps on," replied Juliette in a voice that sounded strangely hoarse.

He shook his head. "No. You need daylight. You need daylight," he repeated, throwing his head back as if he were expecting a shower of light.

"Soliman . . ."

"You know," he said, reading her thoughts, "there are still gardens. They exist here."

He had placed a hand on his forehead, which he moved down to his torso, over his heart.

"How did you know . . . ?"

"The tea. I can't drink it without thinking of them."

Juliette drank some more. She experienced a strange inner calm, which spread as the scalding liquid trickled down her throat. She felt curiously at home here. That didn't mean that all her questions had been answered—how could those simple words "they exist here" have such power? She no longer lived in fairy tales or, like him, in books. Not quite.

But maybe she could learn to live with her questions.

14.

When the man in the green hat pushed open the office door, Juliette sneezed. So as to create a clearer path for visitors, she'd just moved the entire *Human Comedy* by Balzac onto a shelf that looked robust enough to house it—once she'd removed the series of noir fiction, which migrated to the mantelpiece. The hearth was already blocked by a pile of travel books, including the very curious *Travels of Ali Bey in Morocco, Tripoli, Cyprus, Egypt, Arabia, Syria and Turkey, Between the Years 1803 and 1807* published in 1816. The cloud of dust looked almost solid, and the man removed one of his gloves to push it aside, as he would have done a curtain dividing the room.

"Good day, mademoiselle," he said in a fluting voice, which contrasted with his portliness and almost stern expression.

He froze, frowning.

"Where is Soliman?"

He looked surprised and slightly annoyed. Juliette straightened up and rubbed her hands on her jeans. Which was pointless. She was covered in dust from head to toe.

"He's gone away for a while," she replied cautiously.

"Away."

He didn't echo the word in disbelief; no, he simply repeated it, chewed it, like a strange and exotic food. He did this several times, then swept the room with his gaze and, having spotted an empty chair, made his way over to it and dusted it carefully before sitting down, pinching the crease in his trousers to ensure that they fell straight. That done, he looked up and gazed amiably at Juliette.

"Soliman never goes away."

He stated this as if it were a fact.

"I . . . he . . ."

Embarrassed, Juliette started twisting the end of her sleeve. She was wearing a long, very tatty, red sweater. She'd extracted it from the pile that morning because she was in need of comfort. It had been raining nonstop since Soliman had left; Zaide had a cold and was crotchety; in the courtyard a pipe had broken, releasing a persistent smell of rotten eggs. When she'd looked at herself in the little mirror next to the shower, the red sweater had made her feel a bit warmer. But right now, it couldn't protect her from her own shyness.

She surreptitiously pinched the flesh of her arm.

The man in the green hat. The man from the Métro, the insect book, the rustling paper. There, in the office, among the often short-lived towers of book spines and fore edges, multicolored or varying shades of ivory ranging from off-white to mustard yellow. In flesh and blood.

It was as if a character from a novel had slipped out of his book to speak to her.

"He had some difficulties . . . he needed to sort out," she managed to say. "Out of town. I'm minding the shop. Temporarily, of course."

Oh God, was she going to keep yammering on? She stopped talking, her cheeks burning, and became absorbed in contemplating the worn but comfortable sneakers she kept for major clear-up days. To be honest, that was her day-to-day life since she'd been living there, or mostly. She felt surrounded, watched, almost under attack from all these books—where had they come from, anyway? What apparently inexhaustible source supplied the towers, columns, piles, and boxes that seemed to multiply each day? She found some in front of the high iron gate every time she put her nose outside; stumbled over bulging shopping bags that had sometimes burst open, overflowing baskets, stacks tied with string, a wide elastic band, and even, once or twice, a red ribbon that gave these anonymous donations an old-fashioned and rather quixotic aura.

Quixotic, yes. Everything here was quixotic, almost too much so. It was all too much; she wouldn't be able to stand it much longer. She needed a less rarefied atmosphere, less filled with knowledge and stories and plots and subtle dialogues, all of which she explained in a rush, beginning to sob, to the man in the green hat who, disconcerted, removed his hat, tapped her awkwardly on the shoulder, and ended up putting his arms around her and cradling her like a child.

"It's all right, it's all right," he repeated like a mantra.

"No," sniffed Juliette. "I'm rubbish. Soliman trusted me, and I can't do anything. Not even tidy up . . . all this."

"Tidy up?"

He began to laugh. A strange, rusty sort of laugh. Perhaps he hadn't laughed for a long time, thought Juliette, as she rummaged in her pockets for a tissue. She wiped her eyes, blew her nose vigorously, and straightened up.

"I'm so sorry."

"Why?"

"Um . . . because . . . we don't know one another. You must think I'm a real drama queen."

A smile spread over the man's broad face. A smile that also crinkled his eyes, whose shiny irises almost disappeared into his eyelids with their pale, delicate skin covered in tiny red speckles.

"You're wrong, young lady. First of all, I don't think you're a drama queen, as you muddleheadedly say. I don't hold it against you, by the way; we are never aware of what we convey when we describe our symptoms or ailments. And secondly, because there won't be a third point, we know one another very well. Much better, in fact, than you yourself think. You know," he added, "you're not the only person who looks to see what people are reading on the Métro."

15

Half an hour later, Juliette and Leonidas—that really was his name, which made her think, irresistibly, of a mountain of Belgian chocolates—shared an almond croissant that was left over from breakfast and an instant coffee, because Juliette refused to touch the complicated machine invented by Soliman to make the black nectar of which he drank at least twelve cups a day. Looking at the green hat sitting atop a dozen English novels, the coat hanging from a stand wedged—it was missing a leg—between the despised works of a bestselling American novelist, the curls of smoke from the pipe which wreathed the ceiling in a blueish canopy, one might have thought that the visitor was the real occupant of the place, and Juliette a nervous trainee over-anxious to do well.

"I must organize all this," she explained. "I don't know whether I'm coming or going. The *passeurs* turn up, I give them a bag of random books grabbed haphazardly . . . wherever I can't move any more, in fact. I feel as if I'm doing everything all wrong. I . . . I don't know how Soliman worked. I mean, how he chose the books."

Leonidas didn't answer this implicit question; he was deep in thought, his brow knitted, drawing on his pipe and puffing out denser and denser clouds of smoke.

"The problem, my dear child, is not so much to know how he chose them, but how he arranged them. And how the books themselves choose to leave."

They spent the rest of the afternoon exploring the office and the big room next door, where Juliette had not yet dared to venture. It was a room with bare walls lit by two skylights just beneath the ceiling, wider than they were tall, which could be partially opened by pulling on a little chain. But the panes were so filthy that the light they let in was only just sufficient to stop Juliette and Leonidas from bumping into each other.

No shelving here, not even those crude bookcases made out of fruit crates that Soliman seemed so fond of. Just books. Books stacked against the walls, two, three, sometimes four rows deep. The center of the room was empty.

"Well," said Leonidas with satisfaction, "it looks as though Soliman had begun the task that you find insurmountable. We'll find a clue here, a guiding principle, so to speak. Most definitely."

And he nodded twice, puffing out a huge smoke ring as he

did so. Juliette ran to pull the nearest window chain to let in a little air.

"A guiding principle."

She tried for once not to give her voice that questioning lilt that would categorize her once and for all as an airhead in the eyes of this rare book connoisseur.

"You see," said Leonidas, "the classification of books has a history that is at least as interesting as that of the books themselves. I once knew a man . . ."

Changing his mind, he went on: "Perhaps I didn't really know him. Let's say I read a book in which he was the main character—but that's a good way of getting to know people, isn't it? Perhaps the best. Well, this man avoided putting on the same shelf two books whose authors didn't get on, even after their deaths . . . Did you know that for having criticized Cicero, Erasmus was sentenced by a Verona judge to pay one hundred crowns to the poor? Shakespeare and Marlowe both accused the other of plagiarism; Louis-Ferdinand Céline called Sartre a 'little shit-crammed piece of filth'; Jules Vallès considered Baudelaire a blusterer. As for Flaubert, he was a master of damning with faint praise: 'What a man Balzac would have been, had he known how to write!' Writing has never prevented people from being jealous, petty, or bitchy. Excuse me; I'm not usually so crude, but there's no other word for it."

Juliette shot him a sidelong glance and began to laugh. This man made her feel better. A benevolent scholar, a sort of uncle like you find in old novels, the kind who sit you on their knee and let you play with the charms on their watch chain when you're little and later give you an alibi when you stay out all night. She wished she could have met him sooner.

He talked about books as if they were living creatures— old friends, occasionally fearsome adversaries, some resembling bolshie adolescents and others elderly ladies working at their needlepoint by the fireside. According to him, bookcases housed grouchy scholars and lovelorn women, wild furies, would-be killers, skinny boys made of paper holding out their hands to delicate girls whose beauty disintegrated as the words to describe it changed. Some books were frisky horses, not yet broken in, that whisked you off on a mad gallop, breathless, clinging to their manes. Others, boats drifting peacefully on a lake under a full moon. Others still, prisons.

He spoke to her of his favorite authors, of Schiller who never wrote without having put rotten apples in his desk drawer to force himself to work faster, and plunged his feet into a basin of iced water to keep himself awake at night; of Marcel Pagnol, so passionate about mechanics that he patented a nut and bolt that couldn't be undone; of Gabriel García Márquez who, to survive while he was writing *One Hundred Years of Solitude*, sold his car, his heater, his blender, and his hair dryer; grammatical errors in Apollinaire, Balzac, Zola, and Rimbaud, errors which he happily forgave them and even noted with a certain relish.

"I love your stories," said Juliette at length. It had been dark for some time; Zaide must be hungry and she herself felt gnaw-ing pangs in her stomach. "But I can't see anything you might call a guiding principle here. I still don't know where to start. With the writers who make grammatical mistakes? With those who have a hobby, a predisposition to madness? With those who traveled, were sedentary, were reclusive?"

Leonidas chewed on the stem of his pipe, and shook his head with a sigh.

"Me neither, to be honest. But it doesn't matter. Go and get some sleep, dear. Tomorrow you may see things in a completely different light." He pondered for a few moments. "Or not."

"That's not very encouraging . . ."

"Nothing is, in life. It's up to us to find encouragement wherever our eye, or our enthusiasm, our passion, our . . . whatever you call it, is able to find it." He patted her cheek in-dulgently. "And you're capable of doing that. I'm certain."

16

The next day, Juliette stayed away from the books and kept the office locked. From the gallery, she saw a *passeur* walk through the gate and attempt to open the glazed door, then press her nose to it, one hand shading her eyes, but Juliette didn't show herself. Zaide was still unwell, a little feverish and drowsy; she had left her with a whole family of rag dolls, clearly made by hand, to which the little girl told unintelligible stories, holding them one by one against her cheek on the pillow.

Looking at the dolls had made Juliette wonder about Zaide's mother. Was she dead? Did the little girl miss her? Was it possible to make up for the absence of a mother? That was a terrifying question given that the only answer that appeared self-evident was *no*. Juliette made herself some tea, an entire potful, poured out a cup, and sat down to drink it as far as possible from the windows and the courtyard walls, far away from the slightest glimpse of the outside. She needed a soft, calm, peaceful cocoon.

Because that was how she'd always lived. Nestling in the

smallest nook she could find. First at her parents' house, in a peaceful suburb where residents considered the noise of a passing scooter an intolerable nuisance; then the little neighborhood primary school, the secondary school two streets away, the vocational college where she'd gained a diploma in commerce, neither enjoying it nor rebelling, then an advanced vocational certificate. She could have gone further, geographically in any case, could have at least moved to the other side of the ring road, not been content with the careers suggested by the little college where her mother had worked for many years as the principal's efficient and discreet secretary. She hadn't dared. No, actually, she hadn't even wanted to.

She had never been aware that she was afraid, that she feared the world's vastness and diversity, its violence, too. Home, primary school, secondary school, college, and, finally, the agency. The agency located twelve Métro stops from the studio apartment she'd bought with the money her grandmother had left her.

"You won't even have to change platforms," her mother had said approvingly. "That'll make things simple for you, darling."

Juliette's life couldn't have been much simpler. She got up every morning at half past seven, had a shower, sat at the counter of her galley kitchen and ate four crispbreads spread with cream cheese, never any more, drank a glass of apple juice and a cup of tea, and left for work. At midday, she sometimes had lunch with Chloe at the Vietnamese restaurant on the corner—that happened a couple of times a month, except when they'd concluded a juicy sale, in which case they splashed out—otherwise she ate the salad she'd made the previous evening, at the last minute pouring over the dressing from a thoroughly washed little caper jar. She always had an apple on her desk and a packet of Petit Beurre biscuits for tea break. In the evening, she went home, did a little housework, and had dinner in front of the TV. On Friday evenings, she went to the cinema, on Saturdays to the swimming pool, and on Sundays, she had lunch at her parents' and then helped them with the gardening, which filled the time and gave them something to talk about.

Men had occasionally disrupted this routine. But not for long. These men were like running water: they slipped through her fingers; she didn't know what to say to them; her caresses were clumsy; she could tell they were bored beneath her striped duvet, once the shudder of pleasure was over.

When they ditched her, she cried for a few days, buried her nose in her grandmother's scarf, the blue scarf, which she liked to think carried a lingering, even infinitesimal trace of the perfume of the woman who'd knitted it. Of course it didn't. The scarf smelled of synthetic lavender, from the detergent, because it had to be washed from time to time; there was also a whiff of chili, the only dish Juliette occasionally ventured to cook, and the eucalyptus that permeated the tissues of the brand her mother had always bought.

Her mother had died two years earlier, one fine spring evening, as she straightened up triumphantly after weeding a flower bed. The basket containing the wild grasses had been knocked over as she fell, her eyes open, staring at the sky. She hadn't even had time to call her husband, who was thinning out the carrot seedlings close by.

And Juliette missed her. Oh, how she missed her. She had always tried to smooth the ground beneath her daughter's feet, guiding her toward the safest paths, where she would meet neither obstacles nor difficulties. Nor adventures. Nor any other kind of unforeseen event. Nothing that could hurt her deeply, nor anything that could stir her passions, elevate her above herself, above her cautious certainties, her almost cloistered, gentle, humdrum existence.

Why had Juliette allowed herself to be pushed around? Where she came from, almost everyone had let themselves be pushed around—there weren't many rebels. Oh, of course, some of them smoked dope at parties or committed petty offenses, like stealing a CD from the shopping mall or scrawling clumsy graffiti on the wall of a house—but that wasn't rebellion. They all lacked anger. And enthusiasm.

They lacked youth.

Her grandmother, on the other hand, had fought for the right to abortion, for gender equality, for African American civil rights, against nuclear power stations, forced relocations, the massacres in Vietnam, and the war in Iraq. All her life she'd distributed leaflets, gone on demos, signed petitions, and engaged in passionate debate on the ways they could change the world, men, life. Juliette's mother would say with a smile: "Mother is a real cliché." And it was true, she could have come straight out of a film about the seventies, this woman who lived in a little renovated farmhouse in a tiny village in the Pyrenees, wore only natural fibers, had become vegetarian long before the Parisian bohos, read Marx (who on earth read Marx?) and grew cannabis beneath her bedroom window.

And knitted very long scarves for her loved ones.

Juliette's cup was empty. She refilled it and sipped the lukewarm liquid. Soliman's tea had quickly become her favorite. Inhaling the gentle steam, she thought of orange groves, the caress of sea mist, broken white columns, the Italy she'd never seen, apart from in the books she'd read.

Should you, she pondered, staring at a spider that was spinning an almost invisible web in a corner of the ceiling, *travel to the countries you'd loved in books?* Did those countries exist in reality? Virginia Woolf's England had vanished as surely as the Orient of the *One Thousand and One Nights* or the Norway of Sigrid Undset. Thomas Mann's Venice had only survived thanks to Luchino Visconti's sumptuous film. And Russia . . . from the fairy-tale sleigh racing relentlessly across the steppe, you saw wolves, Baba Yaga's cabin on chicken legs, vast snowy plains, dark forests full of danger, enchanted palaces. You danced before the tsar beneath crystal chandeliers, you drank tea from golden bowls, you wore fur hats (how horrid!) made from silver fox pelts.

How much would she find of all that if she took a plane and flew to one of those parts of the world—chaotic regions with shifting borders, where she had covered in a flash almost inconceivable distances, where she had let the centuries roll over her, flitted around among the constellations, spoken to animals and the gods, drunk tea with a rabbit, and tasted hemlock and ambrosia? Where were her companions hiding—Count Pierre from *War and Peace*, the mischievous Alice, Pippi Longstocking, strong enough to lift a horse, Aladdin and Crazy Horse, Cyrano de Bergerac, and all those women she'd dreamed about and whose destinies and passions she'd lived vicariously, at the same time avoiding feeling such emotions herself? Where were Emma Bovary and Anna Karenina, Antigone and Phaedra, Julie and Jane Eyre, Scarlett O'Hara and Lisbeth Salander?

Deep down, she understood Soliman. He at least made no pretense of leading a "normal" life. He had chosen to hide away in a fortress built of books, fragments of which he regularly sent out into the world, like sending messages in bottles across the sea, offerings and gestures of affection destined for kindred spirits, those who, outside the walls, were confronted with real life.

If those words meant anything.

She had a headache at present. Perhaps she'd caught Zaide's cold. Or it was the dust, the kilos of dust she'd inhaled these past few days.

And the Dust Remains. That was the title of a brand-new book she'd seen on top of one of the piles, next to Soliman's worktable. A thriller, judging by the cover. For a rainy day, a cold, when she was feeling a bit down, that was perhaps the best medicine.

It was also a lovely concluding sentence for thoughts and dreams as disjointed as hers.

17

"I want to talk to you about spiders."

The man in the green hat jumped, and his tea spilled into the saucer. Juliette leapt up, a paper napkin in her hand. He brushed her aside, with that same smile, that of the Cheshire Cat in *Alice in Wonderland*, she mused. Simultaneously amiable and distant. In front of him, she felt too young, clumsy, muddleheaded, with "foozling hands," as her grandmother used to say, hands that dropped everything. Even now, she had the impression that she herself had spilled the tea, and perhaps she had, with her odd proposition.

It was because of the book, the book on insects that he read on the Métro—the first time she'd noticed his little game, she'd taken him for a collector or a researcher. She hadn't thought, *completely bonkers, this guy*, but . . . actually, yes, she had thought that.

And now, he was here in front of her.

He came almost every day. Rapped gently on the office door at either 3:47 or 3:49 P.M.—Juliette supposed that this regularity depended on that of the Métro. She was actually starting to miss Line 6, with its familiar landmarks—the finance ministry's speedboat moored under its river porch, the wavy meadow-green curves of the docks building on the opposite bank, the glass roofs of the aboveground stations, and the little nursery school with its tiled roof, a real house standing alone, dwarfed by the increasingly tall apartment buildings surrounding it. She had often gazed at it with a pang of nostalgia; she didn't know why. Then there was the street art of Porte d'Italie, giant murals on the blind gable ends of apartment complexes built in the seventies, the double bridge of Pont de Bir-Hakeim, Passy with its air of a provincial railway station . . . She also missed the strangers to whom she'd given books whose titles were masked by Zaïde's colored card, those people to whom the cover had promised happiness and transformation. She wished she could meet them again, not necessarily to question them—no, reading was something very private and very precious—but to look at them and scan their faces for a clue of a change, of improved well-being or joy, however fleeting. It was stupid, perhaps.

"Is it stupid?" she asked Leonidas after sharing her thoughts with him.

"I thought we were supposed to be talking about spiders . . ."

"That, too. You're an expert on insects . . ."

"Not really. But I never tire of watching them. Nowhere, in my view, does nature's design attain such perfection in any other living being."

"Is that why you always read the same book? On the Métro?"

"Yes. Overwhelmed by my own shameful cowardice and the heartbreak of my unspoken love, I needed comfort. And what is more comforting than the wing structure of the humble *Gryllus campestris*, or field cricket?"

Embarrassed, he fidgeted in his chair.

"That's enough about me. What do you want to start with?"

"Spiders. Why do they climb up drainpipes? Why do they leave a safe place for another which is much more dangerous?"

Leonidas folded and unfolded his pale, carefully manicured hands several times. Each of his nails was polished and perfectly filed.

"The question does not only apply to spiders," he eventually replied. "I could give you a mini lecture on the habits of those arachnids, but my impression is that that is not what you're looking for. Am I correct?"

That unleashed a verbal torrent from Juliette, who couldn't get her words out fast enough. She needed to unburden herself. Her words came tumbling out as she described her confusion in the face of this new life that she was slowly, too slowly, coming to terms with. The crystalline insight that had suddenly shown her the futility of her previous life, her doubts, her fears, and that glimmer of obstinate hope, which was perhaps tucked between the pages of these countless books that were impossible to classify.

"Me, too," she said. "I was covered in dust. It had built up without my being aware of it. Do you understand?"

"I think so," replied Leonidas. "And now?"

She closed her eyes for a moment. "All this"—she raised her arm to indicate the room they were in and beyond, the stockroom, the courtyard, the rickety iron staircase, the rooms that opened onto the gallery, the patch of sky over the neighboring walls and roofs—"blew on me like a great icy wind. I feel naked. I'm cold. I'm afraid."

She heard him move. Gently he placed a hand on her forehead. It reminded her of her grandmother, when she used to visit her in the Pyrenees in winter and she caught a cold from playing for too long out in the snow with wet shoes.

"Congratulations."

Juliette thought she'd misheard. Why was he congratulating her? What had she done to deserve any praise? His hand, so light, did not linger on her skin. She felt it withdraw. Leonidas had gone back to his armchair, which creaked. She didn't dare open her eyes. Not yet. Maybe she'd mistaken irony for sincerity. Maybe . . .

To hell with all the maybes!

She looked at him. Caressed by the blue smoke from his pipe, the man's features rippled, morphed: he was the genie in the lamp, the mischievous goblin who appears in the embers or from a marsh dotted with pale, hopping lights.

Leonidas removed the pipe from his mouth, raised it to his temple, and gently tapped the stem against the side of his head.

"Being afraid is a good thing," he continued calmly. "You are beginning to understand that the great tidy-up that you're planning—and which I do not in any way oppose, believe me—must not take place between these walls."

"Where, then?"

She did not recognize her own voice, which sounded feverish, ardent.

"There. Inside whatever you like to call it—your mind, your head, your heart, your understanding, your consciousness, memories . . . there are plenty of other words. All inadequate, in my view. But that is not what matters."

Supported by the armrests, he leaned toward her slightly.

"It is inside you that all these books must find their place. Inside you. Nowhere else."

"You mean . . . that I must read them all? Every single one?"

Since he said nothing, she wriggled, then folded her arms across her chest protectively.

"And when I've managed that . . . then what?"

Leonidas threw his head back and blew a perfect smoke ring, which he watched dreamily as it unfurled and hit the ceiling.

"You'll forget them."

18

So, she set about reading. A new routine was established: she rose early, made Zaide's breakfast and checked her schoolbag, followed her down the iron staircase which echoed their footsteps, waved her off as she held open the heavy double doors, and then went into the office.

The books were there, waiting for her. Juliette had learned to navigate nimbly between the piles, avoiding the sharp corners of the boxes, and to brush against the bookcases without causing a collapse. She no longer had that suffocating feeling which had previously made her leave the room, then the courtyard, and stride through the streets, her arms folded over her chest to shield herself from the biting wind. The books had become a friendly presence, a sort of soft eiderdown in which she liked to snuggle. She even thought, when she had shut the glazed door behind her, that she heard a sort of buzz, or rather, a vibration, coming from the pages, calling her. She stood still, holding her breath, and waited. The call was louder from this side—no, from the other. It came from the blocked-up hearth or from the dark cranny behind the stepladder. Then she would walk over, cautiously, her hand outstretched to caress the cardboard or worn leather spine. Then she would freeze.

It was *here*. It was *this one*.

Juliette had understood from the beginning that she would not be capable of choosing by herself from among the thousands of books Soliman had accumulated. So she had relied on random selection, already tried and tested during her Métro "missions." You simply had to wait. And stay calm. She couldn't see inside the books—those millions of sentences, words teeming like colonies of ants—but the books could see her. She offered herself to them. Does an easy prey that stays in the open, without trying to run away, arouse the predator's suspicion? Should she really see the books as wild animals dreaming of escaping from their paper cages, ready to throw themselves on her and devour her?

Perhaps. It was of no importance. She wanted to be devoured. A desire that kept her awake at night, drove her out of bed at dawn, and kept her up late under the industrial-style lamp she'd bought at a yard sale in the neighboring avenue—never had she ventured that far before, having contented herself with doing her shopping at the corner grocery store.

She read lying on her stomach on her bed or crouched against the guardrail of the gallery when a ray of sunshine warmed the air; she read propped on her elbows at Soliman's desk and at the kitchen table where she made Zaide's meals;

she read as she flipped the burgers in the frying pan, sautéed mushrooms, or stirred a béchamel sauce. She had even found a position, although somewhat uncomfortable, that enabled her to read while peeling vegetables: she simply had to cradle the book in the crook of her arm and turn the pages with a fork held between her teeth. It was childlike, if you thought about it. She read in the bath, like Chloe's buyer (had she finished *Rebecca?* Had the end of the novel brought the end of her happiness in the apartment whose imperfections had been concealed by the glamour of a love story?), while drinking coffee, and even during visits from the *passeurs*, darting intermittent glances at the page she was on as she nudged a pile of randomly selected books toward them—with an apologetic smile to boot.

Juliette slipped into each story as if into a shiny new skin; her pores imbibed the salt; the perfume used to preserve the suppleness of the limbs of Tahoser, the heroine of Théophile Gautier's 1858 novel *The Romance of a Mummy and Egypt*; the caresses of a stranger encountered aboard a ship. Her ears rang with the boom of gongs, the shrill notes of ancient flutes, hands clapping the rhythm of a dance or applauding a speech, the hissing of waves, rolling smooth pebbles in their blue-green belly. Her eyes stung by the wind, teared up, the heavy face paint of courtesans. Her lips swollen by a thousand kisses. Her fingers covered in invisible gold dust.

From this chaotic reading, she sometimes emerged exhausted, but most often intoxicated. It was no longer she who, at 4:45 P.M., greeted Zaide at the kitchen door: it was Salammbô, Alexander, Sancho Panza, or Calvino's Baron in the Trees, the terrifying Lady Macbeth, Goethe's Charlotte, Catherine Earnshaw—and Heathcliff.

"Tell me the story," the little girl would demand.

And Juliette obliged while spreading butter and jam on three slices of bread, not one more, not one less. Zaide would eat them taking small bites—to draw out the pleasure.

"You're like Soliman," she said on the fifth day. Juliette had noticed that she rarely said "Papa." In her eyes, Zaide was a mini adult, much too earnest sometimes, with a relentless logic.

"Why like Soliman?"

"He always says that he's been to the ends of the earth without moving from his chair. Are you going to do the same? You never go out anymore. You travel inside your head. I couldn't do that."

"But you like stories," replied Juliette, as she plunged her finger into the jar of strawberry jam and licked it, forgetting that she was supposed to set a good example.

"Yes, because . . ."

Zaide wedged her little fist under her chin and began to ponder, knitting her eyebrows. Her expression made the resemblance to her father so striking that Juliette felt emotional—upset. She missed Soliman. She'd had no news from him and was beginning to worry.

"Because the stories make me want to have adventures, too," said Zaide at length. "But I can't, because I'm still too little. But you, you don't like adventures."

"Of course I do!"

"But not real ones. I bet you'd even be afraid on the Métro now."

Juliette raised her right hand, presenting her palm to Zaide.

"Do you want to bet?"

"Depends what we're betting," replied Zaide mischievously. "Adults' bets are no fun. I bet a journey."

Juliette, surprised, raised an eyebrow.

"A journey? But I don't know whether—"

"A journey anywhere. To the building site behind the school. To the big tower blocks I saw one day when I went to the dentist. Anywhere. A journey is when you go to a place you don't know," she added.

"Okay," muttered Juliette, with a lump in her throat.

"What about you, what do you bet?"

Juliette gulped. She couldn't burst into tears in front of this little scrap of a girl who dreamed of faraway places so close to home, as if going beyond her neighborhood was a rare gift.

"The same thing."

Zaide's luminous smile was both a reward and a punishment.

"Tomorrow," Juliette said, "I'll take the Métro again."

"You'll travel the whole length of the line."

"The whole line, I promise. In both directions."

"Several times?"

"Several times, if you like. Why?"

"It's better, you'll see."

This child was just like her father. Too much so.

19

Zaide had been right, Juliette realized, the minute she climbed the steps up to the platform. She was out of breath, and scared. Her shoulder bag was heavy: she'd brought four books, one of them very fat, a Russian novel, probably—she hadn't looked at the title. This weight comforted her, rooted her, amid all the bodies pressing into her. She'd forgotten how crowded it was. Forgotten the sometimes invasive smells, the jostling, the complaining, the eyes averted when a homeless person going from car to car held out their hand or reeled off their plea in a monotonous voice. Forgotten the trepidation, the slamming, the clanking, the dark bellies of the tunnels, the sudden rush of light when the train emerged aboveground, when a ray of sunshine was reflected on a window or a facade, sweeping the faces.

Jammed up against a window, she swayed to the same rhythm as everyone else. She had opened one of her books, a dark thriller which sucked her in like a vortex; from time to time she was jolted out of it when an arm or an elbow dug into her or when the insistent bass from a fellow passenger's headphones mingled with the sounds she imagined as she read.

She read until the last stop, without worrying that she'd miss her station, for once; it was strange, but she actually felt relaxed.

Nation, the final stop. She was the only person left, but she didn't look up from her book. Then the train set off again, in the opposite direction, this time. She hadn't changed seats. And as the city unfurled once more beneath her dreamy gaze, she went back to her character, fair-haired, slim, innocently cruel—and desperate for love. The cellars where he fought superimposed themselves on the trembling images in the rain-lashed windows, contorted, angular, their colors blending to create a fleeting, deceptive shimmer.

The same side of the tracks but the reverse image of the city. Juliette had never taken any notice of it before, but she realized now that she always preferred to have the Seine on her right when she was traveling toward Étoile. She always looked in that direction, and in the evenings she sat so that she could let her gaze roam over the water by turning her head to the left, in the direction of travel.

"You really are crazy."

Juliette jumped. She could have said those words herself—she had perhaps even formulated them in her mind—but the voice was Chloe's.

Chloe, sitting opposite her, in a lime-green suit, with a pink silk scarf and matching lip gloss.

"I've tried to call you hundreds of times."

Juliette blocked out the image of the mobile phone buried under the piles of the nineteenth-century *Grand Larousse* dictionary in fifteen volumes, a rare edition bound in full-grain leather.

"I . . . I think my battery's dead."

It wasn't a lie. Even so, she felt guilty.

"I've been following you for an hour," said Chloe. "You went all the way to Nation, your nose in your book, and now you're coming back. What are you up to? Are you working for the Métro? Are you doing market research, is that it? Do you make notes in the margins? Mind you, I'd rather that, because otherwise you'll end up in the nuthouse, my pet."

Juliette couldn't help smiling. She'd missed Chloe, too. Her wild hair, her irregular teeth, her smile, her killer heels, and her sweeping statements. Even her online shopping addiction and her disastrous taste in clothes—she'd missed all of that.

"You're not mad at me anymore?" she asked, with a note of anxiety in her voice.

"Mad at you? Why?"

"About the books."

"What books? Oh, those . . . of course not. I've moved on, sweetheart. You're the only one to take that seriously . . ."

Chloe suddenly frowned, as if a half-forgotten memory had resurfaced.

"Now that you mention it . . . you left me a book when you quit. On my desk. Is that what you mean?"

"Yes," replied Juliette. "Have you read it?"

"Sort of. I mean, yes." She looked at the other passengers, pouted, then whispered, her hand over her mouth: "Yes, I read it. All of it, even."

"Well?"

Juliette was afraid of sounding too insistent, but she was burning with curiosity.

Chloe adjusted her silk scarf and, puffing herself up, said: "Well, then I handed in my notice."

"You, too?"

"Me, too. And d'you know what, I had the impression that the book approved. That it was encouraging me, even. That it was pushing me. That probably sounds perfectly normal to you, but for me . . ."

She let her voice trail off, her eyes wide, almost frightened, as if it had just dawned on her that she'd unwittingly been the victim of brainwashing or hypnosis.

"So what are you doing now?" asked Juliette, slightly concerned.

With Chloe, nothing would surprise her: perhaps she'd started up an exotic pet–walking business in the wealthy sixteenth arrondissement, specializing in giant lizards; or she was modeling S&M lingerie; organizing tours of the Paris sewers with sound effects; delivering whiskey-Kiri-kiwi cocktails at all hours by bicycle . . .

"I'm learning pastry making. And makeup. And bookkeeping," Chloe reeled off. "It was home staging that gave me the idea, you see. And your book."

"What idea?"

"Wedding planner. Or civil partnerships, or whatever you like, Druid marriages, for example, or wedding benedictions in parachutes with a priest and everything. Organizing things for people and making them happy. You see, if a couple is happy on that day, very happy, they won't want to destroy that happiness, so they'll make an effort. By the way, I need you to make me a list . . ."

"Of my friends who want to get married? Forget it."

"No," said Chloe, with an expression of exasperation. "Books. I'll give every couple a book. It'll be a little extra, the icing on the wedding cake, you get it?"

Yes, Juliette got it. But she was dying to ask another question: "Chloe . . . this is embarrassing but I've forgotten which book I left you. Don't be offended . . . I've been dealing with a lot of books recently"—that was an understatement, she knew—"and I've got everything a bit mixed up."

Her former colleague gave her an indulgent look of the kind usually reserved for three-year-olds and the senile.

"I understand, pet."

She rummaged in her bag and triumphantly brandished a small volume.

"Here it is! It's my lucky charm. I bought five copies so I could be sure always to have one with me."

Juliette looked at the cover, which showed a woman's hand holding a scarlet flower against a blue background, the hand itself emerging from the sleeve of a chunky sweater. Ito Ogawa. *The Restaurant of Love Regained.*

2 0

"Change places. I should make the effort to change places. And not only on the Métro."

Juliette hadn't been able to get those three little phrases out of her head since watching a radiant Chloe walk off down the platform at Pasteur. She passed a couple of newlyweds having themselves photographed in front of a giant poster advertising Chanel N°5. The bride wore a lemon-yellow tulle dress that made her look like a butterfly. To flutter off where? Into a tunnel. That wasn't a positive thought, she told herself. But you couldn't *always* be upbeat. All the same, running into Chloe had done her good. She'd learned, to her amazement, that Monsieur Bernard had closed down the agency. That he'd boxed up his personal coffee maker and his precious cup, and gone off to live in a house on the edge of a forest, somewhere in Ardèche. He had finally understood, he'd told Chloe, what his deepest wish was: to come out of his house in the morning and see a deer run off into the mist.

"Did you leave a book for him, too?" Chloe asked.

"Yes."

"What was it?"

This time Juliette remembered very clearly. *Walden; or, Life in the Woods*, by Henry David Thoreau. She'd been torn between that and a collection of short stories by Italo Calvino. She'd decided on the basis of weight, telling herself that Monsieur Bernard would turn up his nose at a volume that was too slim: he'd always claimed that he liked people "who had substance."

She bounced into the little street where the big rusty gate on the left cast a dark, opaque shadow. She felt good. Maybe she was capable of doing something useful with her life after all, capable of giving people a little energy, a little courage or relief through the books she passed on to them. *No*, she immediately corrected herself. *All of this has nothing to do with you: it was chance. Don't take on airs, my girl.* Those last words had come to her automatically. They sounded like a refrain, words you intone without dwelling on their meaning but which you can't get out of your head.

Who had said that to her? Oh yes, her fourth-grade teacher. Each time she'd succeeded, or thought she'd succeeded at something. The teacher didn't believe in the virtues of what is now called positive reinforcement; no word of encouragement ever left her lips. If you were good at math or drawing, it was genetics, upbringing, or a complex planetary configuration that had decided thus. Chance. Chance. *Don't take on airs, my girl. It's nothing to do with you.*

Juliette reached the door. She put her hand on the cold metal handle.

Maybe it is something to do with me. Just a little.

She repeated it out loud. It was a tiny victory.

Then she noticed a detail, trivial as it was, or at least should have been but wasn't—not at all—that chilled her. The book that kept the door slightly open had disappeared.

It's not possible. It's not possible.

Juliette wasn't able to say those words out loud, but she repeated them to herself over and over, as if to erect a barrier between herself and what Leonidas had just told her, a Leonidas who had lost his Cheshire Cat smile, an ashen Leonidas whose face suddenly resembled a soft cheese running, running, to where it scared her; his face was going to disintegrate before her eyes, spread and vanish between the cracks in the concrete. All that would be left was his hat. What a horrible, strange image, especially right now . . .

She should never have forced her way in through the door; she should never have entered the courtyard, or turned the handle of the office door.

Not to hear *that*.

"When did it happen?"

She had found her voice a little. A mouse squeak.

"Three days ago," replied Leonidas. "It took the hospital awhile to find his address. He'd given another one, a false address, naturally."

"Why a false one?"

"I think he wanted to simply disappear. Maybe he thought he was protecting Zaide. Protecting us. We'll never know."

"But when you go into hospital for an operation, you have to give the name of an emergency contact person," she objected.

"He did." His face creased even more, and he pressed his hands together in a gesture of rage rather than of prayer. "Silvia. The woman who . . . you know . . ."

No, Juliette didn't know. She stared at her own hands, lying motionless on her knees.

"The woman who always had a cookery book with her. The woman who . . . she used to take Line Six as well. Like you. Like me."

"Oh . . ."

"I was in love with her and I never told her. I contented myself with watching her. On the Métro. It was before you, Juliette. You didn't notice, I'm sure. Neither did she."

No, Juliette hadn't noticed. And she didn't want to hear any more—not right now. He understood and apologized: "Forgive me."

She remained silent, merely nodding. Soliman. Soliman was dead. He'd succumbed to the aftereffects of open-heart surgery, a risky operation which he'd put off for far longer than he should have, Leonidas explained. As if he hadn't wanted to give himself the slightest chance, he'd added.

He'd learned all of this at the hospital.

While I was on the Métro. While I was talking to Chloe. When I was happy and a little bit proud of myself, for once.

"What about Zaide?" she asked. "Where's Zaide?"

"Still at school. It's early, you know."

No, Juliette didn't know. She felt as if she had already been sitting there forever, with that thing swelling in her gut, swelling, swelling, which was neither a life nor a promise but rather a death, a recent death that had to be sheltered and cradled, consoled and guided . . .

The word struck her, and she sat up straight. She had promised Zaide a journey—that's really what their bet had been, a promise—and she would keep it. But afterward, wouldn't she be forced to . . . ? She couldn't find the words to express the miserable picture that presented itself, and didn't want to find them, at least not right now.

Leonidas cleared his throat and came over to her.

"Zaide is happy here," he whispered. "But she won't be allowed to stay with us."

With or without his pipe, this man was a sorcerer. Juliette had often thought, since she'd known him, that he could see through a book's cover; and a face was probably just as easy for him to read.

"I know. And yet I can't bear the idea of . . ." No, she couldn't go on.

Once again, he understood.

"Me neither. But the child has a mother, even if Soliman never spoke to you of her."

"I thought . . . that she was dead."

He placed his big hand clumsily on top of Juliette's. She tensed, then allowed herself to accept the comforting warmth of his chubby fingers.

"I know where she lives," he added. "Soliman told me. The day I showed him that Greek spirits were as good as his herbal teas. He was drunk out of his mind, and I regretted it at the time." He bowed his head, his cheeks quivering, then concluded: "Not anymore."

21

Zaide's hand was nothing like Leonidas's: it was so tiny that Juliette was constantly afraid it would slip out of hers. Standing on the suburban train platform, she battled against the gusts of wind whipping up the crumpled papers left under the molded plastic seats, sucking them up and depositing them a little farther down. The passengers who used this suburban line, she thought, must always walk with a stoop to withstand this intermittent onslaught, their foreheads low, their shoulders hunched.

Dourdan-la-Forêt. That was the name of the last stop. Even then you had to make sure not to get onto the branch that went to Saint-Martin d'Étampes and Marolles-en-Hurepoix. Zaide, standing in front of the train map, had repeated that name several times as if it slid over her tongue, leaving a delicious salty taste.

"This is my journey, this is my journey," repeated the little girl rhythmically.

She had just invented a hopscotch game with mysterious

rules that meant she had to hop along the line marking the do-not-step-over area, which she stepped over with every other hop. Juliette, anxious, pulled her back. Zaide froze and glared at her.

"You're like Papa. You're afraid of everything."

Juliette's palm grew moist. For the hundredth time, perhaps, she wondered whether she and Leonidas had done the right thing in concealing the truth from Soliman's daughter. To be honest, not telling Zaide about his death had not been a reasonable, joint decision, nor was it driven by compassion or due to their own grief: they had both simply balked at the difficulty of the task.

Balked, yes. Seeing no further than the wall in front of them, which had to be surmounted—impossible—or knocked down, blindly, without knowing which of the plants that had begun to grow between the stones would die, dry out, or rot, their roots exposed. Zaide was a stubborn little person, with a quick, sometimes sharp tongue; Leonidas thought she was robust, her feet firmly on the ground, long since used to the eccentricities of her father, whom she alternately scolded and indulged.

"Precisely," said Juliette.

She hadn't expanded further. She believed that an entire army of psychologists, who advocated telling the truth as the only way of preventing neurosis, would have demolished her intuition in two seconds.

But this intuition was insistent enough for her to decide, for once, to trust her own instincts. For the time being.

Contrary to what Juliette had believed, Zaide received regular letters from her mother. Over the past few days, she had shown her pages of beautiful, colored drawings surrounded by captions written in a tiny compact handwriting. "This is the house." "A bird in the branches of the pomegranate tree, just outside the kitchen door." "You'd love this walk. We'll do it together one day." "I came across this little donkey on the edge of a field. We talked for ages, he and I. That won't surprise you, I'm sure." Firouzeh signed with a very ornate "F," surrounded by swirls that seemed to float on the paper.

"Firouzeh, that means 'turquoise,'" Zaide had explained. "My mother lives a long way away . . . in a town called Shiraz."

She'd dragged Juliette into her room, pulled out a fat atlas from the pile of books propping up her bed on the door side, and, turning the pages energetically, had pointed at a dot around which she'd drawn a circle with a bright blue marker pen. Juliette had great difficulty holding back the questions she was dying to ask. Why did Zaide's mother write to her in French? Why had Soliman left Iran with his daughter and how long ago? What had happened? And why had Firouzeh, his wife, come back to France a few months ago, but not come to see them? Leonidas hadn't been able to give her any answers. For the past few days he'd been listless, silent. He arrived in the morning, installed himself next to Soliman's desk, and became absorbed in contemplating the photo of Silvia—the woman on Line 6, the one who read recipe books and had chosen one day to ingest her own death, to swallow it, to let herself be carried off by it as if by the surprise of an unknown taste.

Juliette squeezed Zaide's hand tighter. The shiver that ran through her had nothing to do with the biting wind. She was afraid. Of course, Leonidas had written to the little girl's mother—he only had a postal address. Of course, Firouzeh had replied, by snail mail, too, a simple "come" scribbled on a card, slipped into the fold of a sheet of paper covered in sketches that Juliette had gazed at for a long while before showing it to Zaide. A little house whose facade was shaded by the branches of a huge-looking tree, an oak or a linden, probably; window boxes full of orange and red flowers; a painted fence, not white, but green, behind which you could see, against a hazy background of foliage already tinged with autumn, the form of a doe.

Zaide had caressed each of these drawings. She did not even seem surprised . . .

"It's coming! It's coming!" Zaide's backpack jiggled and her braids flew up as she turned her enthralled face toward the far end of the platform. Had she suffered from the seclusion imposed by Soliman, from that sheltered but safe life, going only from the depot to school and back again every day? Juliette had chosen routine, but it had been imposed on Zaide.

Today, though, both of them would experience the thrill of adventure.

Dourdan-la-Forêt . . . yes, this was an adventure. The tiniest departure from routine, if you were open to it, was indeed an adventure.

22

They had some difficulty finding the house. It was two kilometers from the station, in the direction of the woods, the woods that Zaide's mother had painted on the letters sent to her daughter, with overlapping patches of yellow ochre and tender green watercolor. There was a smell of woodsmoke in the air. A bright blue birdhouse served as a letter box; it was planted lopsidedly near a young cherry tree for which it acted as a stake.

"Is this it?" asked Zaide solemnly.

"I think so," replied Juliette.

Suddenly, words had the weight and density of the iron bowls that the men rolled, on a sandy oblong marked out in the courtyard of an apartment building on the other side of the depot wall. For years Zaide must have listened to the sound they made when they banged together, and the furious or delighted exclamations of the *pétanque* players. And Juliette couldn't help looking down at the little girl's mouth, imagining that out of it would come some extraordinary object, like she'd read about in a fairy tale once.

But nothing happened. The ground at the foot of the bird-house had often been trampled; around it, footprints could be seen everywhere, coming from the house, and returning in the same direction. Shallow but clearly defined prints. *Firouzeh has a dancer's feet*, observed Juliette. *She must be small and light—an adult Zaide, in other words.*

Still holding hands, they followed the footprints until they reached the freshly painted door, which was the same color as the birdhouse. Juliette raised her other hand and knocked. The door opened at once: had Firouzeh been watching out for them at one of the low windows either side of the front door? Probably. But the woman who appeared in the doorway bore no resemblance to the one Juliette had pictured: auburn-haired and curvaceous, she wore a big fringed poncho and little, round, steel-framed glasses on her snub nose. Ignoring Juliette, she crouched down beside her daughter and held out her hands, palms upward; Zaide stood stock-still for a moment, looking solemn, then bent down and lay her forehead, just for a moment, on the joined fingers. Perhaps she whispered a word that Juliette guessed at without really hearing.

"*Dead.*"

A truck drove past and the windows rattled. They made a little tinkling sound, and suddenly Juliette saw Soliman busying himself with his makeshift coffee percolator, banging the cups together, while the heady aroma of coffee wafted among the books.

Firouzeh murmured something in Farsi.

Of course Juliette didn't understand that these words were addressed to her, or perhaps to both Zaide and her, any more than she was aware that she was crying, before feeling tears running down her neck and wetting her scarf, the blue one, her favorite.

They had drunk tea and lit the fire, and were sprawled on cushions scattered around the stone hearth. Firouzeh was holding a flyswatter, sending back the sparks thrown out by the logs at the back of the fireplace. Each time, Zaide applauded. Juliette let the honey glide along the handle of her teaspoon, watching the golden liquid shimmer scarlet and green in the light of the flames leaping from the burned-out logs.

Again. And again.

"I didn't want to leave my country," said Firouzeh abruptly. "My mother and father were there. They were getting old. And besides, they'd never liked Soliman. They thought he was a paper man, do you understand? He didn't really exist. You don't know what's going on in his head, my father used to say. But *I* knew, or I thought I did. Love for me, for our daughter, for the mountains—we used to live at the foot of the mountains— for poetry. That's enough to fill a life, don't you think?"

She didn't expect a reply, murmuring as she poked the embers.

"In any case, I believed it because it suited me. Me, poetry . . . it's too complicated, a tortuous road that sometimes leads nowhere. I prefer images, colors. Ultimately, perhaps it's the same thing. Soliman and I argued about it endlessly, and it tired me. I said to him, life isn't an almond: you won't find the best of it by removing the shell and then the skin. But he persisted. That's how he was. He went out less and less; he stayed shut up in one room all day long, that one with the window looking out onto the almond orchard. The same things, he would say, looked at often, observed determinedly, can give us the key to what we are. I don't know what he was seeking, what he wanted . . ."

Firouzeh looked up. Her gaze was fixed, very somber.

"I never understood him. And he never understood me. That's how it is, I suppose, with most couples. They tell each other about themselves with passion, they think they know everything, understand everything, accept everything, and then the first crack appears, the first blow, not necessarily dealt out of spite, but dealt, and everything is shattered . . . and you find yourself naked and alone, next to a stranger who is also naked and alone. It's unbearable."

"He couldn't bear it," said Juliette softly.

"No."

"He left."

"Yes. With Zaide. I was the one who wanted it. She was

closer to him than to me. I knew that everything would be easier for her here. And perhaps for him."

"So why did you leave your house in the end?"

"My parents died. I no longer had anyone back there. When I got here, I could only think of one thing: seeing my daughter again. I almost . . . and then . . ."

Her eyelids closed.

"I wasn't complete. Exile is . . . I don't know how else to explain it. I was no longer complete, and I didn't want to inflict that on Zaide. This emptiness, this anxiety, this 'nothingness' that I couldn't shake off. So I waited. We sold land; we weren't hard up. Back there I had my job. I was a teacher, a French teacher . . . here, I started illustrating children's books. That helps. The money helped Soliman, too, at first."

"Even though he started going around in circles in one room again," Juliette interjected.

"He used to say that one room can contain an entire world."

"Books," murmured Juliette. "Of course." And she began to tell her story.

23

Juliette had been in the little house on the edge of the forest for three days, waiting—for what, she couldn't say. She knew only that this was a cold, peaceful place, incredibly luminous, vast, empty; that she sank into it without resisting, with relief even.

She had cried a lot, at first. Like a child experiencing her first disappointment, an adolescent her first heartbreak. The sight of a cup of coffee made her burst into tears; an old black sweater flung over the back of a chair had her sobbing. It reminded her of the misshapen jumper worn by that familiar, clumsy, gangly form—even though this one was an extra small, whose sleeves had shrunk in the wash, into which Soliman couldn't even have wriggled his long arms.

Firouzeh remained imperturbable, following her with her gaze but not attempting to comfort her, other than to bring her endless cups of tea.

"You could have been English, couldn't you?" said Juliette between sobs, wiping her eyes with the corner of the shawl which Zaide, full of concern, had wrapped around her shoulders. "The English think that tea is the answer to everything. In Agatha Christie's novels—"

"I've never read them," Firouzeh interrupted her lightheartedly. "I told you, I prefer images. Colors. Gestures that caress the paper, the skin . . ."

She put the cup down on the mantelpiece. Her hand was trembling a little.

"His skin . . . Soliman's skin . . . it was olive, but not the same all over, with dark hollows, pale areas . . . a mole . . . and the shape of his thighs . . . I must show you . . . I must draw . . ."

"No," whispered Juliette, staring at the tips of her shoes.

Firouzeh held a hand out toward her.

"Juliette . . . you and he . . . you weren't . . . ?"

"No."

"But you're crying."

"Yes. It's not normal, is that what you mean?" she burst out, suddenly aggressive. "And Zaide isn't crying. Is that normal?"

Firouzeh placed her fingers over Juliette's. It felt as if a woodland bird had just chosen her as a perch, and she found it strangely comforting.

"Normal. I've never understood the meaning of the word. Have you?"

Juliette was silent, and so Firouzeh just stroked her daughter's hair. Zaide had snuggled up to her and was beginning to hum. The melody was surprising, sometimes low to the point of being inaudible—only a vibration of her throat indicated the sound emanating from her—and sometimes high, reedy, and taut like a child's solo. Zaide closed her eyes, put her thumb in her mouth, and fell asleep.

Juliette allowed one last tear to dry on her cheek and gazed at her. She watched the years fade away on a face that was already so young, and saw the little girl morph into the newborn that had lain on her mother's stomach the day she was born.

"I don't know if it's normal," Juliette said after a time. "I feel empty, that's all. My life was filled with trivial things. I didn't like them, well, not really; but they were there, they were enough. And then I met them, the pair of them . . ."

She closed her eyes for a moment.

"I should say the four of them. Soliman, Zaide, the man in the green hat, and the woman who . . . who died, too. Each of them gave me something and, at the same time, they've taken everything away. There's nothing left, do you see? I'm like a shell. I feel the draft blowing through me. I'm cold."

"You're lucky," said Firouzeh slowly. "Me, I'm full of this child I've been reunited with. Of her absence. Of her presence. Of the death that has brought us together. It's the end of my journey . . . for the time being. But don't think I regret it."

She extricated herself gently from the little arms embracing her, walked over to the windows, and opened both. A gust of strong wind blew into the room, and blue flames leapt up from the embers.

"The wind," she said, "the wind . . . Get out of here, Juliette, go and breathe. Go and listen to it. You've stayed shut up inside with your books for too long. Like him. Books and people need to travel."

Zaide hadn't woken up. She shifted slightly all the same, like a kitten stretching in the clutches of a dream.

Firouzeh had been right about her. Juliette did have a book in her pocket. She could feel its shape against her as she walked around the house with tiny steps.

I'm pathetic. Like an old lady.

It did her good to laugh at herself. As did feeling the soft cover through the fabric. It was a book by Maya Angelou, *Letter to My Daughter*, which she'd stuffed in her pocket at the last minute, before leaving. Because it was within reach on top of a pile. Because it wasn't very big, and their two bags were already heavy. (She wasn't used to choosing her reading material by weight: that was a first. But not necessarily a bad idea, she said to herself: it was a way of classifying the books she hadn't yet tackled—fat fireside tomes or long, lazy holiday reads, picnic books, short-story collections for brief, frequent journeys, themed anthologies to dip into on each break, when the telephone is quiet, when your colleagues are at lunch, when you're propped on your elbows on the counter of a café, drinking a double espresso that you eke out until you reach the end of the section you're reading.)

During the journey, she'd merely flicked through the book;

Zaide had kept pointing out sights glimpsed in passing—the red-and-white-striped roof of a circus big top, an oblong pond where ducks were swimming, a bonfire in a garden, its smoke spiraling up in the sunshine. And all those roads and cars, all going somewhere, like them.

"People are going places, it's crazy," Zaide declared. "All the time."

Just then, Juliette's finger slid between two pages, and she read:

I am a black woman
tall as a cypress

She hadn't managed to read on. She'd picked up the slim volume again in the evening, on the living-room sofa where Firouzeh had heaped pillows and a warm duvet for her. It wasn't a poem by the author; it was by Mari Evans—Mari Evans, whose name she'd immediately googled, to learn—squinting, enlarging the page on her smartphone—that she'd been born in 1919 in Ohio, and that that poem, "I Am a Black Woman," had become a sort of rallying cry for many African American women, including Maya Angelou, who herself had fought for black women throughout her life. Michelle Obama had said that for her it had been the power of Maya Angelou's words that had led a little black girl from the poor neighborhoods of Chicago to the White House.

In her book, Angelou cited this poem as giving heart to African Americans in general and women in particular.

And its last lines were:

Look
   on me and be
renewed.

24

I'm not black. I'm not tall as a cypress. I'm not strong. I'm not impervious. And yet I, too, have things to face. So look and be renewed . . . that would be good, yes. But look at what? And where?

Juliette looked up. She was wearing an oversize beige parka, borrowed from Firouzeh, and felt a bit ridiculous, like a child who's rifled through her mother's wardrobe. The blue scarf, wound twice around her neck, muffled her up to her nose. She breathed in the biting air through the stitches that her grandmother's fingers had knitted one by one. Suddenly, she could see those fingers very clearly: slightly knobbly, her hands covered with those blemishes known by the rather unpleasant name of liver spots. Her grandmother's fingers—and those of Silvia, the woman on the Métro, the one who'd decided to leave a life in which there was maybe no one left for whom she could knit scarves or simply work to make life a little more joyful—had now ceased all movement, and that stillness distorted the rhythm of the world, Juliette could feel it. She had to find something, and quickly, to set it right again.

Idiot.

She felt ridiculous. Honestly, who on earth did she think she was? She was unhappy, or rather, dejected, and she'd felt like that before Soliman's death. She couldn't find her place in the world—so what? Her place was where life had put her, wasn't it, where she herself had chosen to hide away, close to the ground. And that was that . . .

And that was that . . .

It was depressing, but that was the truth.

She carried on walking aimlessly, pushing aside the dark, wet branches of a huge willow that reached the ground and blocked her path. Shards of broken flowerpots rolled underfoot, between the heaps of rotting mown grass and the little vegetable garden that Firouzeh had marked out with lengths of string stretched between stakes. There was already a small radish bed, in a corner, and winter lettuces. The freshly dug earth looked rich and dark, warm no doubt if she were to plunge her fingers into it.

A few meters away, beyond the rusty garden fence, Juliette saw a derelict shed made of planks turned gray with age. The roof had caved in, and between the planks that had come away and were broken in places she could glimpse a bright yellow patch. As yellow as the throat of a hummingbird. As the fluffy mimosa flowers with their heady perfume, which she used to buy years ago for her mother who dreamed every winter of Nice and the Riviera, but didn't want to budge an inch from her home.

Her hand on the galvanized wire, Juliette pushed the sagging fence down and climbed over, praying that Firouzeh's parka wouldn't get caught on one of the barbs. Once on the other side, she jumped over a little ditch filled with stagnant water, then zigzagged between the clumps of nettles and barley-colored stems. This section of the property seemed to have been abandoned long ago and must have served as a rubbish dump: the legs of an ironing board stood in the middle of a heap of plastic containers filled with blackish liquid; stacks of rotten fabric covered a rickety stepladder. On top of the lot, she saw an iron stuck in an ancient washtub and a hat—yes, a red, spangled carnival hat, which looked brand-new.

The shed door was jammed with several sheets of corrugated iron, but an entire side of the wall was nearly flattened. A green tarpaulin covered the vehicle sitting inside, standing on chocks—like during the war, thought Juliette, when there was no gasoline left. But in those days, there weren't any yellow cars, or were there? Of course there were. (The world wasn't in black-and-white, despite what she'd believed when she'd seen *The Trip Across Paris* for the first time. In her defense, she must have been only six years old.)

She grabbed a corner of the tarpaulin and yanked it. A few bricks, placed on the roof, clattered down. She stepped to one side to avoid them and yanked again with all her strength. Sweat ran down her neck onto her back. Where did this sudden boldness come from? Juliette didn't even know whether this land belonged to Firouzeh, or whether she rented it—the legal owner might at any moment burst out from the woods with a loaded hunting rifle and—

The tarpaulin ripped and fell back limply. On its inner side, moss made maps of improbable continents. Small animals scurried away amid a rustling of dried leaves—field mice, perhaps. She had disturbed a little living space with well-established habits, the patiently built nest between the axles harboring maybe a litter of tiny pink blind creatures—no, it wasn't the right season. Could she be certain? Not really. You couldn't be certain of anything that happened in the countryside, when you've spent so much time on Line 6 of the Paris Métro. She tended to imagine the lives of animals in their burrows like someone who has acquired all their knowledge from watching the Disney version of *Alice in Wonderland*.

She yanked again, dislodging a few more bricks, and at last it appeared before her, as inoffensive and appealing as a big toy, but a lot dirtier.

A minibus. Yellow.

"Is it yours?"

A breathless Juliette had burst into the studio where Firouzeh was building a totem with Zaide. They had placed several lumps of wood on top of one another, split logs with tender pink hearts, and were dribbling different-colored paints over them.

"Then," explained Zaide, "we'll make eyes out of modeling clay. And eyebrows. And a mouth, so it can palaver."

She repeated the word "palaver" several times, seeking Juliette's admiration.

"Palaver's a good word. Did you know it?"

Juliette shook her head. "You're very clever."

Zaide pulled a modest face and turned over the log she was holding in her paint-stained hands. A crimson stream soaked into its fibers.

"The wood's bleeding," she crooned, "it's going to die."

Firouzeh tapped her shoulder. "The tree died when it was cut down. But this piece is going to stay alive."

"Why?"

"Because of the palavering and the wishes. You see, when we've put together these two logs, there'll be a hollow, there, just at the join. When you're sad, or when you have a special wish, you can write it on a piece of paper and slip it inside. My grandfather taught me to do that."

"And then what happens?"

Firouzeh looked up and her eyes met Juliette's.

"The wood eats everything. Sorrows, hopes, everything. It keeps them safe. It leaves our hands free to release us from them or to make them come true. It depends what you tell it."

"So," Juliette broke in, "is it yours?"

Firouzeh showed no surprise. She simply took the time to put the lids back on the paint pots on the shelf before turning toward the window. Behind the filthy panes, it was possible to make out the dead colors of the wild patch, the shed and its deformed shape, barely visible in the fog.

"Yes. I mean no," she replied. "It's yours. If you want it."

25

"You really want to do that."

It wasn't a question. Leonidas, sitting in Soliman's armchair, surrounded by a haze of pipe smoke as always, simply wanted to be sure that he had understood the hasty, garbled speech Juliette had made.

"It's a good idea, don't you think? I never managed to do what Soliman asked me to do: follow someone and study them carefully to find out what book they needed, working out which one would give them the hope, or the energy, or the anger they were lacking. This way, I'll have lots of books in the minibus, and I'll go and see people in the villages, and I'll take the time to get to know them, at least a little. It will be easier. To advise them, I mean. To find the right book. For them."

The man in the green hat—which was still perched on top of his head—took his pipe out of his mouth and gazed pensively at the bowl.

"Does what Soliman wanted matter so much to you? Did it ever occur to you that he was simply mad, and the rest of us with him? You don't see us *passeurs* as some kind of . . . healers of the soul, doctors who wander around with their bags of medicines?"

"Well . . ."

How to tell him that yes, it was like that in a way? That she had ended up believing, no, being convinced, that all the world's diseases—and all the remedies—were concealed between the covers of books? That in books you found betrayal, solitude, murder, madness, rage—everything that could grab you by the throat and ruin your life, not to mention others' lives, and that sometimes crying over printed pages could save a person's life? That finding your soul mate in the middle of an African novel or a Korean tale helped you realize the extent to which human beings suffer from the same ills, the extent to which we are alike, and that it is perhaps possible to talk to one another—to smile, caress one another, exchange signs of recognition, any signs—to try to harm others less from day to day? But Juliette was afraid of reading on Leonidas's face an expression of condescension because, yes, all that was pop psychology.

And yet she believed it.

So she waited on the street corner for the breakdown vehicle from Dourdan-la-Forêt, paid the exorbitant sum the driver demanded without wincing, watched him unload the minibus—which at present looked like a wreck and nothing like the ball of sunshine she thought she'd seen shining back there, in the tumbledown shed, wreathed in the deceptive magic of the fog.

She called the nearest garage—out of the question, this time, to bankrupt herself with a long-distance charge—asked for an estimate, pulled a face, went up to the attic to retrieve the last pots of yellow paint, bought some detergent, and set to work.

Leonidas had brought out a garden chair and was sitting in front of the glazed door of the office, watching her. Every so often, he brought her an almond croissant and an instant coffee—they had given up trying to get Soliman's contraption to work—nodded solemnly, and went back and sat down. The other *passeurs* had stopped coming. The rumors must have got around; they circulated even faster than the books, with their words released from the weight of print. Perhaps, mused Juliette, scrubbing the mold-encrusted bonnet, the story of the world as she knew it was one big rumor that some people had taken the trouble to set down in writing, and which would continue to evolve, again and again, until the end. The fact remained that they were alone.

With their ghosts.

And the bus, which sloughed off its dead skin like a snake clinging to a shrub, began to gleam again. It seemed to take up more and more room in the little courtyard.

"It's so big," muttered Leonidas, unable to conceal a certain admiration. "Now what do we do?"

Juliette was standing next to him, proud of her efforts, struggling to peel off her rubber gloves. The bodywork was still yellow, several different yellows because she'd had to buy more paint, and the fad for buttercup yellow had long since been replaced by one for canary or grapefruit yellow. There was still some of the original color left, on the bonnet, where the bodywork had been best protected. She was sorry that Zaide wasn't there to paint flowers on the doors, as she'd done in the room Soliman had invited Juliette to move into just a few weeks earlier. But Zaide would not return to the depot. Not for a while, anyway. In the meantime, Leonidas was going to live there—his pension, he joked, could well do without having to cover rent. He wanted to rebuild the network of *passeurs*, to carry on, in short, and also . . .

"Boats need a home port," he said that day, looking at the newly painted bus. "And that is a boat. Not a racing yacht for sure—there's nothing streamlined about it. It's even rather plump. It looks like a child's toy. It reminds me of that Beatles song, 'Yellow Submarine,' do you know it? That's what we should call it."

Juliette began to laugh.

"You know the Beatles?" she asked, incredulous.

"Of course. Even if I were a hundred, I'd know them. You're the one who's not of your era, Juliette. And you're marvelous that way. Although I won't tell you to stay as you are, because it's the opposite of what you want. But keep that little . . . I must be getting old; I can't find my words. I can't put my finger on what it is."

"Neither can I," murmured Juliette.

He smiled at her—a slightly wistful smile, but full of kindness.

"Just as well, really."

26

She set off one rainy morning. It wasn't what she'd planned, or imagined: the *Yellow Submarine*—the *Y.S.*, as she called it, for short—looked dull under the dismal gray clouds, so low they grazed the rooftops. She had spent almost a week choosing the books that would be crammed onto the shelves screwed to the metal walls.

"I'll come back every so often to restock," Juliette had said.

She'd laughed, and so had Leonidas. He added: "People will bring you books, wherever you stop. The ones they want to get rid of, most likely."

"Or, on the contrary, the ones they love most . . . don't be such a pessimist! Isn't it better to give away a book one loves?"

Leonidas nodded indulgently.

"That's true. But I think you're deluding yourself, Juliette."

She said nothing for a moment and looked pensive, perhaps sad.

"You're right. But ultimately, I prefer that. Staying a bit stupid."

After a long argument, they'd decided, for this first trip, not to include series, because Juliette wasn't certain to return to such-and-such a village to drop off volume two, three, or twelve. She wanted to preserve her freedom, that precious freedom which she was only just beginning to learn to handle. Proust would remain in the depot for now, and so would Balzac, Zola, Tolkien, the books of Charlotte Delbo, even though she loved them, Lian Hearn's Otori trilogy, the complete *Diary of Virginia Woolf*, the three volumes of Herbjørg Wassmo's *Dina's Book*, *Tales of the City* by Armistead Maupin, Marion Zimmer Bradley's Darkover series, *1Q84* by Haruki Murakami, *The Man Without Qualities* by Robert Musil, and all the famous family sagas that wouldn't fit into the palm of a hand. What remained were the solitary works, fat ones, thin ones, medium-size ones, those whose spines were already split from having been opened and sometimes left facedown on a table or a sofa, the rare ones whose binding still smelled of cardboard and new leather, those that had been covered like schoolbooks in the old days. Juliette still remembered the unruly plastic film that wouldn't stay put, that constrained the spine of the book and left your hands sticky.

There, too, she had to make a choice. It was no easier than classifying them.

"I wonder . . ."

Sitting on a box full of paperback novels, Juliette bit her lip—all heroines in romances did that—frowning.

"The thing is, the *Y.S.* isn't a mobile library. There are already lots of those. So I don't need to worry about catering to all tastes, all ages, all readers' interests . . . or do I? What do you think? Leonidas?"

"Nothing."

"What do you mean, nothing?"

Leonidas, who was flicking through his precious book on insects—which he took everywhere with him in his briefcase—darted a severe look at Juliette over his half-moon glasses.

"Why am I supposed to have an opinion on everything? My choice would inevitably be different from yours. And right now, it's yours that matters."

"But I have to take into account what the readers like, too," insisted Juliette.

"Do you think so?"

"Yes."

"So go back into the Métro and take notes. You've already started that, haven't you?"

Juliette nodded. Yes, she'd started a sort of list—especially of repeats. Books she'd seen in several pairs of hands, more than once in the week.

"But they're not necessarily the best ones," she argued. "I'm not going to be taken in by . . . um . . . publishers' hype."

Leonidas shrugged as he fondly ran his magnifying glass

over a color plate illustrating the *Empusa pennata*, noting its bipectinated antennae so closely resembling tiny dry twigs.

"It takes a little of everything to create a world," he said placidly. "Even a world of books."

Those journeys on the Métro were tinged with a sense of farewell. As well as titles of novels, Juliette brought back images, lovingly recorded with care: a fresco she'd never noticed before, depicting a woman in a tutu jumping, her legs folded under her, eyes closed, in front of a cityscape against a backdrop of cotton-candy-pink clouds—as if she were dancing among the stars, or falling, or spiraling up in a dream; pigeons—females, she decided—strutting along the glass canopies at Dupleix station; the fleeting image of a gilded dome; the graceful curve of the track just before Sèvres-Lecourbe; an oval-shaped apartment building, another one round as a pancake, and another clad in gray slates like scales, which shimmered with green, blue, and purple reflections when the train passed; a roof garden; the Sacré-Coeur in the distance; the hefty barges cleaving the river, others moored, decked out like gardens with bamboo hedges in huge planters and little tables, chairs, seats . . . Juliette alighted at almost every station, changing carriages, watching people's faces, waiting, without admitting it to herself, for a sign. Someone, surely, would smile at her or wish her well, like at New Year, or say something mysterious that she would take years to understand—but nothing happened. One last time, she ignored the escalators, climbed up the gray steps glinting with mica particles, and walked off into the rain.

Again, it was in the rain, a persistent drizzle, that she carted out the boxes full of the books she'd decided to take with her, or that had surreptitiously placed themselves in her line of vision—she no longer knew, and ultimately it didn't matter. If she had learned one thing, it was this: with books, there were always surprises.

The shelves the local carpenter had built (not without a certain amount of mockery) had brackets to prevent the books from falling off as she rounded the first bend in the road. Once filled, they gave the interior of the bus a warm, quirky feel.

"It's better than Soliman's office," observed Leonidas, amazed. "More . . . intimate, in a way."

Juliette agreed: if she hadn't had to get behind the wheel, she'd have happily snuggled up under the tartan blanket with a cup of tea and one of the many books lining the walls. They created a tapestry of colorful and abstract patterns, the reds and apple greens making a splash among the classic ivory, pale yellow, and gray-blue covers.

In the little remaining space, she piled everything she would need: that tartan blanket, a rolled-up futon, a sleeping bag, several folding stools, a lidded basket containing crockery and kitchen utensils, a little camping stove, and some nonperishable foods. And a flashlight, of course, to be able to read at night. A torch that she'd hang from a hook that would sway, projecting moving shadows onto the rows of books.

Leonidas was worried about her, a woman on her own, on the road . . . Juliette saw the newspaper headlines dancing in his round eyes as he pictured her dismembered under a bush. A few minutes before her departure, he stood in front of her, arms dangling, looking dejected. She wedged her first-aid kit under the driver's seat, turned around, and hugged him.

"I'll be careful. I promise."

"You don't even know where you're going," he complained in an uncharacteristic voice.

"Is that so important, do you think?"

He hugged her tight, awkwardly.

"Maybe. It's silly, I know. But it would reassure me."

Suddenly, his face lit up.

"Wait for me. Just a minute, please, Juliette."

He turned around and almost ran in the direction of the office. Juliette started hopping from one foot to the other. Her stomach was knotted with anxiety, but she was in a hurry now, in a hurry to get the goodbyes over with, in a hurry to make the engine rumble and drive through the gray streets into the unknown. Leonidas came bounding back. Under his raincoat there was a strange bump on his stomach. When he stopped in front of her, panting, he reached under the fabric and pulled out three books.

"The first one is from Zaïde," he explained. "I almost forgot, I'm sorry. She'd have been furious with me."

It was a copy of Rudyard Kipling's *Just So Stories*. Touched, Juliette leafed through it. Soliman's daughter had carefully cut out the illustrations, which she'd replaced with her own drawings. A purple crocodile was pulling the trunk of a baby elephant with huge terrified eyes and outsize feet; a slant-eyed whale rose out of the sea; a cat, its tail raised, was wandering toward the horizon where something closely resembling a little yellow truck was vanishing in the distance.

"*I am the cat who walks by himself, and all places are alike to me*," murmured Juliette, a lump in her throat. "Is that how she sees me, do you think?"

"Do you?"

Without giving her time to reply, he took the book of stories from her hands. Juliette held her breath: the second book, she recognized. She had often seen it lying in the lap of the woman with the gentle face, Silvia, the one who had chosen to die, to nurse her memories no longer.

A recipe book, written in Italian, tattered, stained, often used.

"I so regret not having spoken to her," he said softly. "We could have grown old together. Made one another happy. I didn't dare. I'm angry with myself. No, don't say anything, Juliette. Please."

His lower lip was trembling a little. Juliette kept still. He was right. *Don't speak, don't move. Let him pour out his heart.*

"Soliman told me a little about her," he went on. "She had no family, apart from a nephew over in Italy. In Lecce. That's below Brindisi . . . in the far south. She had once told him that this book was the only thing she had to bequeath. That these pages contained her entire youth, and her country: the colors, the songs, the sorrows, too, the grieving, the laughter, the dances, the loves. Everything. So . . . I didn't dare ask you but . . . I'd like . . ."

Juliette understood.

"Me to take it to him?"

"Yes. And the last one," he added hurriedly, "is a French–Italian conversation manual. I found it yesterday in one of the drawers of Soliman's desk. Maybe he himself intended to go to Lecce; we'll never know. And the newsstand on the corner sells maps. I can go and get you one if you like."

"Are you so certain that I'm going to say yes? And how am I supposed to recognize her nephew? Do you know his name, at least?"

"No. But I know he has a little restaurant near the Via Novantacinquesimo Reggimento Fanteria. It's a bit of a mouthful, I know, so I've written it down for you."

"There must be dozens of restaurants there!" she exclaimed.

She looked down at the cover with its faded colors. The vegetables, the plump red peppers. The cheese cut with a single knife stroke. And, in the background, the ghost of a hill, an olive tree, a low house. *You can want to enter into the land-*

scape of a book, she reminded herself. *To linger there. To start a new life.*

"I'll recognize him," she announced suddenly.

"Yes," echoed Leonidas. "You'll recognize him, I'm certain you will."

EPILOGUE

JULIETTE

For the last time—the last time that year, at least; I couldn't see any further ahead—I followed Line 6, but not riding the Métro. The *Y.S.* drove parallel to the viaduct of the overground section, keeping pace with a train that had left Saint-Jacques station just as I pulled away from the traffic lights. At Bercy, it plunged back underground again, while I turned right toward Avenue du Général-Michel-Bizot, heading out of Paris and the entrance to the A6 motorway. I intended to stay on it as far as Mâcon; there, I'd leave the main roads once and for all and drive down to Lecce via the smallest country roads possible. I didn't know how long this journey would take, and I was excited at the thought of it. I had sublet my studio flat when I moved into Soliman's place, so I had a little money, enough to keep the tank filled and to buy food—and for everything else, I'd manage. I had a jerrican and a bag of clothes, a windbreaker and boots, Leonidas's French–Italian conversation manual, and Zaide's present. And books, lots of books.

I also had names dancing in my head—Alessandria, Firenze, Perugia, Terni—and the one that always made me laugh because it made me think of the only board game my parents ever played: Monopoli. Each day, I'd throw my dice to move forward a few kilometers, but I wouldn't be content to make my way round a board and keep passing the same squares; I'd go forward, I'd really go forward. Toward what, I had no idea. After Lecce, maybe I'd go to the sea. Then I'd drive up the length of the boot by a different route; I'd go and visit the lakes of northern Italy and continue eastward, or to the north. The world was absolutely vast.

I suddenly recalled an evening with Zaide—one of our last evenings together at the depot. She had filled a glass salad bowl with water and placed it on the kitchen table. She turned on all the lights and then brandished a pipette.

"Look," she said.

She was just like her father when her eyes lit up with that special radiance, that of a magician who is about to transform illusion into wonder and make you think about the reality you are witnessing. She was so like him that I felt, once more, tears prick my eyes, a lump rise from my stomach and lodge in my throat.

The little girl dipped her pipette in the water, then held it up to the lightbulb dangling over the table.

In the liquid drop that was slowly stretching, she had captured the entire room: the window and its four panes with the waning daylight, the chest covered with a red rug, the sink with the handle of a saucepan poking out, the big photo tacked to the wall showing an almond tree bowed under a storm, its blossoms torn off, blown away, tiny angel flights or sacrificed lives.

"The world's tiny . . . it's a pity we can't keep droplets for all the beautiful things we see. And for people. I'd love that. I'd put them in . . ." Zaide broke off, shaking her head. "No. You can't put them anywhere. But it's beautiful."

I whispered, "Yes, the world is beautiful," discreetly pressing a finger into the corner of my eye—wretched tears!

The world seemed to me like a Russian doll: I was in the bus, which was a little world of its own and which was driving in a vast yet tiny world. Behind me, sitting on the floor, was a woman with a sweet, tired face, a man whose overly long arms protruded from the too-short sleeves of his black sweater, a laughing girl in a flounced dress, and then there was my mother, too, panic-stricken—I was going to leave the safety zone she'd created for me for good. There were all the men I'd thought I'd loved, and all my paper friends, but they were brandishing glasses of champagne and absinthe, they were the broke, alcoholic poets, sad dreamers, lovers, unsavory characters, as my father would have said (my last visit to him had not gone very well; but there's no point going into detail). My family.

A few hundred meters farther on, the train I'd been following left me behind when I stopped at a pedestrian crossing. I watched all those strangers flash past, people I must have glimpsed at least once on the Métro, some of whom I recognized—from their walking stick, the way they turned up their coat collar, muffling themselves up to their glasses, or from the backpack that swayed between their shoulder blades to the rocking of the train.

And then I saw her. The girl who read romances, the girl with pretty breasts in tight polo-neck sweaters, moss green, powder pink, honey mustard. The one who always started to cry at page 247, when all seems lost.

"It's the best moment," Soliman had said.

I had the feeling, for my part, of having gone beyond page 247—not by much. Just a little. Just enough to savor the radiant smile of the girl who had a fat novel wedged under her arm, four hundred and fifty pages, by the look of it.

Just before crossing, she put the book down on a bench. Without looking at it. Then she started running.

The drivers behind me were growing impatient, but I still hadn't pulled away. I couldn't take my eyes off the book, from which a cardboard bookmark protruded, stiff and white with a beveled edge.

I switched on my hazard lights and parked by the left-hand curb. Three or four cars passed me in a cacophony of hooting and swearing out of hastily lowered windows. I didn't even turn my head; I didn't want to, not at all, at the sight of their furious expressions and contorted mouths. So let them hurry. I had all the time in the world.

I got out of the Y.S. and went over to the bench. I didn't

look at the title of the novel; what intrigued me was the bookmark. I slid my finger between the smooth pages. Page 309.

> Manuela pressed her forehead against the silky fabric of the dinner jacket.
>
> "I'm so tired," she whispered. The huge arms encircled her.
>
> "Come," whispered in her ear the voice she heard every night in her dreams. "Come."

Disconcerted, I let the novel fall shut on the little cardboard rectangle. The reader from Line 6 had abandoned her book before the end—there was nearly a third of the story unread: how many ups and downs still, partings, betrayals, returns, kisses, torrid embraces, and perhaps a closing scene on the deck of an ocean liner sailing to America, with two silhouettes at the prow, a laugh borne away by the wind, or a silence, because you can be as overwhelmed by joy as you can by an irretrievable loss.

So there I was, mentally writing the end of the book, and that was perhaps the reason it was there, on that bench, for me to pick up, so that I could fill it with romantic dreams that no one dares admit to, stories you consume in secret, feeling slightly ashamed. But she wasn't ashamed, that girl who had so often cried in front of me, on the Métro, and now she was running in the street, toward whom, toward what, I'll never know, and she had left her book there on the bench.

I placed my hand on the cover. It was already a little damp. I hoped that someone would find it before the pages got wet. I wasn't going to take it. For the time being, I had decided to give, not to take. There's a time and a place for everything.

The *Yellow Submarine* was there, waiting for me. I was clutching the keys in my left hand.

Before going back to it, I bent down and removed the bookmark, which I slipped under my sweater, against my skin. The beveled corner dug into my breast, and I enjoyed feeling that prick—that small stab of pain.

I knew that it would stay with me. For a long time.

SUGGESTED READING

The citations in chapter 7 are from:

The Odyssey, Book 14
Violette Leduc, *L'Affamée*
Thomas Hardy, *Tess of the d'Urbervilles*
Arthur Rimbaud, "L'Éternité"
Marie NDiaye, *Three Strong Women*
Sandrine Collette, *Nothing But Dust*

On the Y.S.'s first trip, Juliette travels with:

The Ice Palace by Tarjei Vesaas
Owls Do Cry by Janet Frame
The Wonderful Adventure of Nils Holgersson by Selma Lagerlöf
My Brother and His Brother by Håkan Lindqvist
Sula by Toni Morrison
The Voyage Out by Virginia Woolf
The Glass Bead Game by Hermann Hesse

Mudwoman by Joyce Carol Oates

The Magic Mountain by Thomas Mann

Break of Day by Colette

Seedtime by Philippe Jaccottet

La voix sombre by Ryoko Sekiguchi

The Human Race by Robert Antelme

The Ratcatcher: A Lyrical Satire by Marina Tsvetaeva

Dangerous Liaisons by Pierre Choderlos de Laclos

Last Things by Umberto Saba

I Know Why the Caged Bird Sings by Maya Angelou

One Hundred Years of Solitude by Gabriel García Márquez

Sweet Days of Discipline by Fleur Jaeggy

Lolly Willowes by Sylvia Townsend Warner

The Guernsey Literary and Potato Peel Pie Society by Mary
    Ann Shaffer and Annie Barrows

The Book of Sand by Jorge Luis Borges

The Pillow Book by Sei Shōnagon

Nedjma by Kateb Yacine

Vowels of the Sea: Amers by Saint-John Perse

Interview with the Vampire by Anne Rice

We Need to Talk About Kevin by Lionel Shriver

In the Mothers' Land by Elisabeth Vonarburg

A Suspicious River by Laura Kasischke

Hopscotch by Julio Cortázar

The Day Before Happiness by Erri De Luca

Un petit cheval et une voiture by Anne Perry-Bouquet

The Lion by Joseph Kessel

The Torment of Others by Val McDermid
Ice by Anna Kavan
Les Pierres sauvages by Fernand Pouillon
Gare du Nord by Abdelkader Djemaï
Milena by Margarete Buber-Neumann
Letters to a Young Poet by Rainer Maria Rilke
Beggars of Life by Jim Tully
Bartleby, the Scrivener by Herman Melville
Snow Country by Yasunari Kawabata
Ask the Dust by John Fante
Dalva by Jim Harrison
Journal by Mireille Havet
The Suns of Independence by Ahmadou Kourouma

This list, although extremely incomplete—it wasn't possible to mention all the books on board the *Y.S.*—is given haphazardly, as it was compiled. That is the charm of many libraries. You can add your own favorites, your discoveries, all the books you'd recommend to a friend—or to your worst enemy, so they will no longer be so, if the magic works. Or even to the person sitting next to you on the train.

ABOUT THE AUTHOR

Christine Féret-Fleury is an author based in France. *The Girl Who Reads on the Métro* is her first book to be translated into English and is being published around the world.